Come Back to Me

When Esmé Rogers meets Luke Carlisle in 1987, she never expected to end up on board the Titanic for its maiden voyage from Southampton to New York in 1912. But what started with confusion and questions turns into the greatest love of her life.

As the date of the ill-fated sinking of the ocean liner approaches, Esmé questions whether or not she should try and change history. However, one question keeps coming back to haunt her: Does she survive?

With frigid waters and a predestined collision on the horizon, can she change the fate of those she loves?

Dedication

Mum

1939 - 2019

My Mother Kept a Garden by Anon

My Mother kept a garden.

A garden of the heart;

She planted all the good things,

That gave my life it's start.

She turned me to the sunshine,

And encouraged me to dream:

Fostering and nurturing

The seeds of self-esteem.

And when the winds and rains came,

She protected me enough;

But not too much, she knew I'd need

To stand up strong and tough.

Her constant good example,

Always taught me right from wrong;

Markers for my pathway

To last my whole life long.

I am my Mother's garden,

I am her legacy.

And I hope today she feels the love,

Reflected back from me.

Chapter One

1987

THE THROB BEHIND MY TEMPLES CAUSED ME TO flinch. Because of how sensitive I'd become, the sound of people murmuring and talking, as well as loud laughter, silverware clinking, and even a dish breaking, was exacerbating the pain. I desperately needed some peace and quiet to calm my racing mind. The crowded restaurant felt suffocating, and I longed for a tranquil setting where I could find solace and relief from the escalating pain. I couldn't take it any longer.

Jake, my fiancé, was aware of my distress, but instead of pitying me, he insisted we continue on our path. The business dinner could result in him becoming the new partner at the law firm where he currently worked full-time. Despite my deteriorating condition, I mustered the courage to put on a brave face, knowing how important this opportunity was for Jake's career. However, as the pain became more intense, I silently hoped that Jake would recognize the gravity of my situation and prioritize my well-being over his professional ambitions.

My fiancé had changed in New York, and I no longer felt like I was a part of a couple. His long hours at the firm had created a schism between us, to the point where I no longer knew him. I yearned for the days when we could spend quality time together, laughing and dreaming. It was disheartening to see how his work had taken precedence over our relationship, leaving me feeling isolated and disconnected.

The idea of ending our relationship had crossed my mind a few times. Jake, on the other hand, would do something romantic, and I would forget about leaving. But I knew that these fleeting moments of romance couldn't solve the underlying problem. I wished for a partner who cared about our relationship and made me feel valued, rather than someone to bring out to business dinners. My heart was troubled by the uncertainty of our future together, leaving me conflicted and torn. I wondered if I was settling for less than I deserved, and if staying in the relationship would eventually stifle my personal growth and happiness. I desired clarity and the courage to make a decision that was truly in line with my own needs and desires.

I rubbed my temples once more as I surveyed the dimly lit room. The shelves of the small, family-run Italian restaurant were adorned with jars of decorative oils, dried pastas, and hot peppers. The restaurant's bustling atmosphere gave me a sense of familiarity and comfort. It brought back memories of the vibrant energy I had always felt in my own Italian American family gatherings. I felt lonely as I watched the chaotic yet harmonious dance of the staff.

My gaze was drawn across the restaurant to an elderly gentleman in a wheelchair. I wondered about his story because he had a warm smile on his face. Perhaps he, too, felt nostalgic in this bustling Italian setting, longing for the days when he could join in the lively conversations and laughter. He looked at me from beneath lowered lids. He'd once been a strong man, but his build and height had deteriorated with age. Something about him made me feel at ease. Had we ever met?

Although the pain in my temples had begun to fade, when I shook my head to clear the fog, pain shot down into my neck. I flinched and returned my gaze to my dinner companions, who continued to ignore me.

I returned my gaze to the elderly man, who whispered something to his companion—a granddaughter, perhaps, or even a great granddaughter? The woman was young and appeared to be around my age—twenty-five. Her long, graceful curls hung over her shoulders in her thick blonde hair. She was small and flowery.

While her companion continued to speak with her, the woman glanced over, holding my confused gaze. I sensed the man's urgency as he pushed the young woman in my direction.

"Esmé honey, Bill just asked you a question," Jake prompted.

I ignored him and waited, knowing I was the young woman's final destination.

Jake tried to capture my attention for a brief moment before giving up and mumbling something to his guests.

As she approached, the young woman tugged nervously on her slim fingers, her teeth gnawing at her bottom lip. She came to a complete stop right in front of me. I offered an encouraging smile in response to the young woman's nervousness.

"I know this is an unusual request." The young lady

cast a glance at her companion before returning her gaze to me. "My name is Sienna Taylor, and I was hoping you wouldn't mind coming over to my table to meet Luke. I look after him. He's been agitated most of the day. He says he knew you a long time ago."

Sienna cast another glance behind her. Tears sparkled in her eyes as she focused on me once again. "Please?" she pleaded. "I'm sure he's imagining you." She laughed softly. "I mean you can't be much older than me, except to hear him talk, it's as though he knew you when he was our age."

As the woman continued, I reached out and squeezed Sienna's hand in comfort.

Sienna said, "In his own mind, Luke believes what he's saying, and the thing is, I need him to calm down. He's 102 years old, and...*well,* his health is failing." Her fingers twisted together. "I know he's done well to get to such an age, and I've grown to love him." She smiled wetly.

My interest was piqued as I listened. What made this even more intriguing was my inability to shake the feeling that there was more to the story. I wondered if me and the old man had a deeper connection, something that could explain the sense of familiarity I felt. I had a good memory for faces, and his wasn't one that came to mind, but I had a feeling I knew him.

I stood, suddenly realizing I'd been sat staring, and walked beside Sienna toward the elderly man, as if in a trance. "Can I ask you, his name?"

"Luke Carlisle."

Luke Carlisle....How do I know you?

I drew a chair closer to his side as I approached. I forced myself to lift my gaze to his face. His eyes were cornflower blue and glittered with an unidentified emotion.

Luke reached out to me with trembling hands, so I quickly covered his with my own. That's when I noticed he was clutching something in his hand and attempting to pass it to me.

I grasped what turned out to be an aged gold locket on a thin chain. Sienna gasped behind her, causing me to turn toward Sienna.

"Luke's son, William, once told me that Luke wears a locket around his neck and has done so since the Titanic sank in 1912. William suspected it belonged to a woman his father had met on the ship. When I asked Luke about it, he always had a distant look on his face." Sienna fixed her gaze on the locket. "This is the first time I've seen it from around his neck," she said quietly, looking at Luke in awe.

I frowned, my gaze fixed on the antique locket, which was encrusted with intricate engravings of orange blossom flowers and swirling scrolls. I was perplexed as to why Luke had given it to me when it clearly meant so much to him.

My palm was sealed around the locket as old hands closed over mine. "I don't know how," he said quietly, "but I promised I would find you." Luke coughed after swallowing. Sienna assisted him in taking a sip of water, and the coughing stopped.

"I don't understand." I moved in closer. "How do I know you?"

"You know Luke?" Sienna inquired, kneeling beside his chair, her gaze fixed on my face.

"I honestly don't remember," I said as I licked my dry lips, "but everything about him hints at a memory."

Luke gave a soft smile and nodded. "You need to come back to me."

"What? Luke?"

He ignored Sienna and forced me to look him in the eyes. "Come back to me..." His eyes drooped and he fell silent as soon as the words left his mouth.

In a panic, I looked at Sienna, who shook her head. "Don't be concerned. He's sound asleep." Sienna took the chair next to me and stared at the locket I held in my hands.

"I don't understand any of this," I admitted, pleadingly looking at Sienna. "What did he mean when he said, 'come back to me', I wonder?"

Sienna nodded her head, as if she'd decided. "Come to his home tomorrow morning." She opened her purse and handed me a gold-embossed business card after rummaging around. "He's more awake first thing in the morning, so hopefully he'll make more sense."

I trembled inside. "What time?"

"Any time after seven-thirty."

I nodded and walked back to where my enraged fiancé waited.

ALTHOUGH I DESPISED THE SILENCE BETWEEN JAKE and myself, I appreciated it. My head continued to throb behind my temples. But it hadn't stopped since my unexpected encounter with Luke Carlisle.

Luke Carlisle had been adamant about knowing me. It completely perplexed me. But there was something strange about him. I sensed it in the restaurant. What exactly had it been? His tone of voice? His gaze had been unnervingly clear and focused on my face. As I reflected on our meeting, I couldn't shake the feeling that Luke Carlisle held the key to a long-forgotten part of my past. The intensity in his gaze had triggered a long-forgotten memory, one that remained just out of reach, leaving me with an unsettling curiosity about our relationship.

He was a puzzle that I had to figure out. I wouldn't be able to settle until I knew more about Luke and how I was connected to him. I was certain there was a link. When he touched my hand, it was there. Luke had pleaded with his eyes, and I had been disappointed in myself—I hadn't fully comprehended what he had asked of me. His words 'come back to me' stayed with me.

My attention was drawn to the lovely locket in my hand, but I was startled when Jake stormed out of the bathroom, showered, and was ready for bed. He was tall and medium-built, with tawny-gold hair on his head. His square jaw was visibly tense right now. He looked at me, angry and frustrated, his eyes searching for answers. I wondered if he'd noticed my brief moment of connection with Luke. I quickly hid the locket behind my back as I approached, hoping to avoid any questions about its significance.

After closing his side of the closet with another thump, he sighed. He turned to me, his hazel eyes brimming with rage. "Would it hurt you to show your support for my career once in a while?" He shifted his weight to the bed. "Instead of being indifferent," he hissed.

He yanked the large throw pillows off the bed and crawled between the sheets. "I know you despise business dinners, but tonight was crucial," he continued.

"I apologize, Jake. My migraine interfered, and then the elderly man diverted my attention." I rubbed my brow and frowned. "He claims to know who I am, but I don't see how. I don't recall him. But there's something about him..." I began to stutter.

I looked at Jake as I took my nightgown from the armchair by the bed. "I really am sorry." I was. Regardless of how our lives had diverged, I'd let him down.

I entered the bathroom, locked the door, and looked in the mirror while resting my hands on the vanity. My body was slim, and my auburn hair fell to my waist. My emerald-green eyes shone brightly from my delicate face. Despite my tiredness and headache, my face shone with peach undertones.

My gaze returned to the chain and locket, my fingers caressing the engraved design. I picked it up with my delicate fingers and slipped it around my neck. I attempted to open the locket, but it refused to budge. Perhaps it had become stuck with age. I gently yanked on the locket, hoping to loosen it, but it remained firmly closed.

Wondering about the locket, I quickly changed into my nightgown, the locket hung delightfully between my breasts.

The weight of the locket against my skin provided a comforting presence as I lay in bed five minutes later. *What secrets and stories did the locket hold from generations past?* I fell asleep, intrigued, and determined to solve the mystery of the stubbornly closed locket in the morning.

As I stood on the stoop of the townhouse where Luke Carlisle lived with his caregiver, my stomach rolled. I pressed my palm against the black front door, my head bowed as I summoned the courage to knock.

The brass door knocker called to me, but before I could reach for it, the door swung open. Sienna stood there, her eyes red and watery. "I wasn't sure if you planned on knocking or not," Sienna said.

Sienna backed up into the house, leaving me no choice but to follow, albeit cautiously.

The chandelier that dropped three floors was the first thing I noticed when I stepped inside the spacious entryway. My gaze was drawn to the curved staircase leading to the ground floor and the dark hardwood flooring beneath my booted feet. I took in the decor as I followed Sienna upstairs. The paintings were all classic portraits and landscapes, lending an old-world feel to the home. As I walked through the hallways, I felt a sense of nostalgia, admiring the intricate details of each piece. It was as if I had stepped back in time, surrounded by the splendor of another era.

The further we walked, I had a feeling something had happened after I left the restaurant because the woman beside me appeared pale and sad. I reached out and touched Sienna's arm. "What's happened?"

Sienna turned slowly, but she couldn't stop a tear from falling down her cheek. "I had to contact the doctor. He doesn't have much time left."

I snatched my hand back and clutched my chest, stunned.

"Old age," Sienna added, a sad smile on her face. "He's waiting for you."

I followed her down a short hallway lined with more antique paintings until we came to a halt outside a dark-paneled door.

"I'll let you go in alone." Sienna stepped back and, without another word, returned the way we'd come, leaving me to ponder my appearance.

I paused for a moment, my heart racing with excitement. I took a deep breath and reached for the door, unsure of what to expect.

When I stepped into the room, I discovered Luke propped up in the middle of a king-sized bed. Dark furniture dominated the room. A machine beeped next to the bed, and another hissed with oxygen.

"You came," Luke said, his voice tired but hopeful.

Luke patted the bed with a frail hand, so I moved to sit close beside him. My gaze was drawn to his, and I asked him the question on my mind. "Why are you familiar to me?"

For a few minutes, he closed his eyes and focused on his breathing. "We met," he said, with a whimsical smile on his lips, "a very long time ago." Paused. "You were everything to me, and then you disappeared."

My confusion must have been visible on my face. "You think I'm insane. I'm just an elderly man with a wandering mind."

"No." I dropped my purse to the floor and reached for his hand. I was overcome with emotion the moment we touched. My mind searched for something - something related to this man - but I didn't have time to grasp it before it was gone. "I believe you, but I'm not sure why? Or how?" In awe, I shook my head.

"I've spent a long time waiting for this moment, and now, I can finally rest in peace."

"But—" I trailed off, overwhelmed with emotion.

"Right now, nothing makes sense to you. I know." Sadness seeped from him before he caught his breath. "I know because when you left me, I was heartbroken and out of my mind - and then I realized—"

"Realized what?" I bent closer that I could see every wrinkle on a face I recognized but couldn't put my finger on. It was his gaze and the way he looked at me.

"I knew I had to wait to see you again - to give you this." He lifted his other hand, which was too weak to move very far, so I leaned over and took an old plated photograph from his grasp.

It was much heavier than a photographic print today. It was brown in color and featured an image of a couple in evening attire. I looked closely, my surprise visible as I mumbled words that made no sense, finally meeting Luke's damp eyes. "That can't be me. How is this even possible? It has to be a family member?"

My gaze returned to the image. This time, I took notice of the man in the photograph, who was dressed for the occasion. While I had no way of knowing, his clothing appeared to be expensive. They were a good fit for his tall, muscular frame. His short dark hair was neatly swept back from his face, but it was his eyes that drew my attention—like now. He was attractive, with full lips and a secret expression. His affection for the woman on his arm was visible even on the old photographic plate.

"I'm tired now," mumbled Luke.

I felt my heart crack as I blinked at the man in the bed. I had no idea what was going on or why I experienced so much emotion. How could I? After all, I'd only met the man the night before - I couldn't recall ever meeting him before. Luke opened his eyes ten minutes later and looked me in the eyes. "Would you please put my hand to your face? I'd like to touch you one last time."

When I moved his hand until his palm covered my cheek, I caught my breath and tears slid down my lashes.

His palm remained steady as he brushed his thumb over my skin. "Just as I remember."

When his arm began to tremble, I gently repositioned it on the bed while keeping his hand in mine.

"I'm not going to wake up again," he said quietly, clutching my hand. Then he said the words I was certain would haunt me for the rest of my life, "I never stopped loving you. It was always you. Come back to me, Esmé."

Luke Carlisle breathed his last.

Chapter Three

1987

"You need to snap out of this," Jake hissed, his anger evident in every word. "You've been acting like a ghost since that old man died two weeks ago. You're supposed to be here with me, but are you? You don't care if I get the promotion or not. You're uninterested in anything!" In his rage, he paced back and forth like a sentry.

I only paid him half attention as I counted down the minutes until he left for work. I was curious about what Luke had given me and Jake wasted precious minutes of my time with his ranting. I knew he had every right to be angry. I'd let him down. He hadn't stopped going on about that night and it grated on my nerves.

The last few weeks had been a blur for me as I grieved the loss of Luke. I'd felt his love for me and, though I didn't understand it, my heart had shattered when Luke died while I held his hand. I couldn't understand the melancholy that had gripped me - it wouldn't let go. It was as if I had lost my parents all over again, making me feel guilty. I couldn't figure out why my grief over Luke's death was so intense.

I hadn't been able to concentrate on anything else since Luke gave me the picture of him and the woman who had to be a relative of mine. I needed answers because the image couldn't possibly be of me. It was unthinkable. Except Luke thought it was me. I couldn't get rid of the nagging feeling that there was more to this mysterious connection than I realized. The weight of uncertainty and confusion only fueled my desire to discover the truth, propelling me into a never-ending search for answers that consumed my every waking moment.

Sienna had been taken aback when she discovered the photograph Luke had given me. Especially after she had given the woman in the image her full attention. At Luke's funeral, Sienna had asked Luke's Grandson, David, but he'd never seen the photograph before. So, I hoped that when I visited Frederick Fitzwilliam later in the day, he'd have answers. The man was the fifth generation of his family to run the photography store. I reasoned that if anyone could date the glass plate, he could.

"Dammit Esmé!"

I was taken aback.

Jake looked at me before the door slammed shut behind him.

Overcome with sadness, I fingered the locket around my neck with a huge sigh of relief. Nothing had made sense to me since meeting Luke. The man was a complete mystery.

I checked the time and determined Jake had already left the building, so I turned and dashed for the hall closet. I'd hidden everything I would need for the day while Jake had been in the bathroom. He'd been following me around like a hawk for weeks, and I'd had enough.

I needed to call it quits with Jake because I didn't think either of us wanted to go through with it any longer. I didn't love him, and I doubted I ever had.

My thoughts, however, were not for Jake, but for Luke. I didn't think I'd be able to move on with my life until I had answers, whether I stayed with Jake or not.

Sighing heavily, I exited my apartment and jumped into the cab that the doorman had summoned for me.

I gave the driver the address and found myself outside the photography store twenty minutes later.

I checked the chained sign to make sure I was in the right place. I was.

The black awning appeared to be well past its sell-by date, and the windows needed a good cleaning.

As sadness settled into my shoulders, my excitement for receiving answers began to fade. The neglected property didn't appear to have been occupied in a long time, implying that dear *Frederick* would not be present.

"Are you looking for me?"

I stumbled and turned quickly, catching myself on a wrought-iron lamppost.

The man dashed over and grabbed at my arm. " I apologize for startling you." He let go of me as quickly as he'd touched me and nodded toward the closed store. "It's me. Fitzwilliam Frederick. I assumed you were a customer." He shrugged and took a step back, giving me room.

"Esmé Rogers." I wrapped an arm around my stomach and said, "I'm attempting to date an old photograph. Maybe find out where it was taken. It's a glass plate."

"Ah! Please accompany me." Excitedly, the man rubbed his hands together. "I haven't had a challenge in years." He fiddled with his keys until he found the correct one on the fourth try.

I inhaled deeply and followed him through the squeaky doorway. The musty odor and layers of dust confirmed my suspicions - no one had been in the store in a long time. Disappointment washed over me as I pondered what I could possibly learn from the musty business.

My gaze returned to Frederick. He was in his thirties, not particularly tall, with pale, receding, overlong hair and a slight paunch. He appeared friendly enough, but only time would tell.

At the very least, Sienna knew I was at the store in case I suddenly disappeared. The other woman would undoubtedly call for news - I hoped to have something to tell her.

"Let me get some lights on." The room was filled with light as soon as he finished speaking. It was so bright that Thomas Edison would have been pleased.

"I require light in order to work. You'll grow accustomed to it." He tossed his satchel to the floor and motioned me over to an old desk.

I ran my fingers along the edge and, surprisingly, found no dust. "Nice desk," I said, trying to hide my embarrassment at being discovered.

I cleared my throat and removed the plate from

the protective case I'd placed it in. I hesitated as I handed it over, not sure why. I did want answer, didn't I?

Frederick exclaimed in delight as he took it from my hands. He slid it onto the light box. "Where did you get this?" he asked, his eyes wide.

"Someone left it to me."

"What?" He jumped out of his chair and approached the photograph so closely that his nose almost touched it. "You have a remarkable resemblance to this woman," he said.

I hid my unease behind a smile as my stomach quivered. "So, I've been told. Other than the likeness I have for her, is there anything else you notice?" I asked, clearing my throat.

"Hmm." He held an eyeglass up to his eye and looked at the photograph. It fell out seconds later. He sank heavily into the chair behind him. "That can't be right."

"What is it?" I leaned in close.

"Let me look again." As he took a long look at the photograph, he picked up the eyeglass, his hands shook, and his body tensed.

"You say someone left you this?" He looked at me with interest.

I provided him with a brief explanation. "The man

who gave me this died only five minutes later. He was over a century old." I blinked back tears. "Please," I begged, "I need to know about this photograph."

"This photo was taken on the RMS Titanic. I'm not sure of the exact date, but the liner sailed on her maiden voyage on April 10th, 1912. She collided with an iceberg on April 14th and sank to the ocean floor a few hours later, on April 15th. Between those dates, this photograph was taken." I sat in stunned silence, while Frederick grinned with delight. "It can't be seen with the naked eye, but with the eyeglass, I can just make out the writing on the door that they're standing beside." He indicated with a large finger. "See?"

He handed me the eyeglass, which I took in my trembling hand as Frederick turned the photograph around. I looked up, butterflies in my stomach, and saw what he had. The RMS Titanic was written in gold letters.

With a thud, I sat back down, my heart racing. "That can't be." Even as I said those words, I knew the photograph was from 1912. Sienna had told me about Luke being a Titanic survivor, so I should have known.

But who was the lady in the photo? I needed answers. "Can you look at the woman and tell me if there is any marking on her *neck*?" I asked, passing the eyeglass back.

Frederick gave me an odd look before taking the eyeglass and burying his face in the photograph once more. He frowned and looked me in the eyes. "How did you know?"

I took a deep, trembling breath and slowly drew the silky scarf away from my neck. "I didn't, but I expected to have answers. Despite this, I'm still as perplexed as ever. Is this the mark on the photograph?"

"Yes," he said, perplexed. "Now, I'm confused."

I locked my gaze on him and then jumped up, feeling compelled to flee. "I need to go," I exclaimed, panicked. "Thank you for your help." I quickly slipped the photograph into my pocket. "How much do I owe you?"

"You owe me nothing, but you can't leave right now," he begged as he followed me to the door. "I need to know more!"

"I'm really sorry." I turned and bolted from the store. I didn't stop running for three blocks until I was out of breath. My mind raced with questions about the mysterious photograph as I leaned against a lamp-post. After a brief moment of reflection, I realized I had more questions. I gasped and moved back and forth slowly, forcing my breathing to even out. Only then did I enter the phone booth.

Sienna answered the phone on the first ring. "I've been waiting for your call."

I was at a loss for what to say to Sienna. It wasn't like I could tell Sienna about the woman's small beauty mark—the same mark on the right side of my own neck. In any case, not over the phone. My thoughts raced around the possibilities and the questions they raised.

"Esmé, are you still there?"

"April 1912," I exclaimed. "Sienna, the photograph was taken on board the RMS Titanic."

"But - Oh! Can he tell you anything about the lady?"

I let Sienna's question hang in the air, refusing to respond. Then I noticed where I was and what was across the street - *The New York Public Library*. They'd be able to look up people, and they'd have access to all of the newspaper archives dating back to 1912. Wouldn't they?

AS I WALKED INTO THE LIBRARY, I FELT A NERVOUS flutter in my stomach. I hadn't been there since I moved to New York. My favorite bookstore was close to the apartment building, so I never made it down to the library.

I smiled as I looked around for the reference section and noticed a group of children surrounding a large table to the left. They were engaged in conversation with one of the librarians while their teacher kept a close eye on them. I yearned for the carefree days of my childhood.

I made my way slowly to the long front desk, where the librarians and their assistants were at work. The whir of a copy machine drew her attention, and once it had discarded the last piece of paper, the loud tick of the clock became irritating.

My gaze wandered around the library, taking in the rows of neatly organized bookshelves and the cozy reading nooks strewn about. I recalled fondly the hours I had spent as a child lost in the pages of my favorite books in the town library.

My attention was drawn to a throat clearing. "Can I help you?" enquired a middle-aged librarian.

I smiled. "Please can you tell me where I might find a list of survivors from the Titanic?"

The woman tsked, clearly irritated. "Really? Why?"

"I just really need to see the list." I wanted to scream at the woman.

Her jaw clenched. "It could take a while to find."

I stood firm and simply stared at the woman. Finally, the woman sighed in annoyance. "Follow me then."

I rolled my eyes but didn't say anything. There was no rush for the woman, whereas I was irritated. I wondered why the woman seemed so hesitant to help me as we walked through the library.

Before instructing me to sit in front of a microfilm machine, the woman led me through rows and rows of thick dictionaries, encyclopedias, atlases, and what appeared to be historical texts.

"Give me a few minutes to find the relevant information." The woman stomped away, her feet thudding on the hardwood floor, her rage visible.

Hopefully, she would return.

A loud sneeze startled me, followed by a whispered, "Excuse me." I chuckled silently after two more quick sneezes.

The grumpy librarian returned after five minutes. "This has the information. Do you know how to operate the machine?" she asked, in a very unhelpful manner.

"Yes." No, but I'd figure it out eventually.

"Very well," she exclaimed.

I breathed a sigh of relief when the woman left and had the machine up and running in five minutes.

I was almost afraid of what I would discover, but I had to know if I had been on the Titanic with Luke for some inexplicable reason. Was I insane to listen to him? I hoped not, because he'd undoubtedly believed what he'd said.

As the names of the first-class passengers began to appear, my stomach fluttered. My heart skipped a beat when I read 'Carlisle, Luke'. My machine-operating hand froze.

Everyone said Luke was on the ship, so seeing his name shouldn't come as a surprise. It was, however, the case.

My ears filled with blood as I searched for the letter R. The name Rogers did not appear on the list. As a first-class passenger, no. I was temporarily blinded by tears as I was overcome with disappointment. I'd hoped to find my name, strange as it was.

I quickly checked the second- and third-class passenger lists, but they were empty. No Rogers. Nothing.

My hands trembled as I placed the film back into the container. I quickly took a tissue from my purse, wiped my face, and composed myself before thanking the librarian and leaving.

I collapsed on the steps of the library outside. My mind raced with Luke-related thoughts. He had been so insistent on me finding him. The photograph he'd given me was taken on the ship, and it was of me. It had to be because the similarities were striking. So why hadn't my name appeared on the lists?

It made no sense. Nothing made sense to me any longer.

Chapter Four

1987

"Do you think I'm crazy?" I asked once I'd finished telling Sienna about the photograph, including how the woman had the same beauty mark as myself.

"I would have said yes if I hadn't seen Luke's reaction to you. But he was adamant that he knew you. He said he'd been waiting for you to return to him for years. I'm not sure what you're talking about. But he thought you were – were - the woman in the photo." Sienna came to a halt, her brow furrowed as she attempted to make sense of the situation. "It's definitely strange," she finally replied, "but sometimes people have unexplainable connections. Perhaps there's more to this image than meets the eye. Perhaps it's worth digging deeper to learn the truth behind Luke's conviction."

I observed Sienna's bottom lip as she moved over to the dining table in the old town house. I noticed old, dark wood furniture everywhere I looked. The worn carpet and faded wallpaper suggested a bygone era, adding to the mystery of the location. It would have been costly at the time. Sienna stroked the table with her small hand before taking up a large, brown box that appeared to be as old as the furniture. It was tied with a ribbon whose color appeared to have faded over time.

As she moved slowly over to the sofa and placed the box on top of the coffee table, Sienna's gaze was drawn to mine. "I found this at the back of Luke's closet." She took the seat directly across from me. "The name tag says Esmé Rogers. I'm assuming that's you. The box and tag were covered in a really thick layer of dust. They'd probably been there for years."

I moved closer, knelt, and hesitated before fingering the tag.

Darling Esmé,
Wear this and come back to me.
Luke, yours forever my love.

My face paled as I felt all the blood rush from my head. I became dizzy. My mind raced as I grabbed the coffee table in front of me.

"I wish I knew what was going on." I took a deep breath and looked up at Sienna. "I searched the archives for Luke, and he was there on the passenger list, but - I wasn't."

I shifted to my feet and moved slowly over to the oval window on trembling legs. I turned to face the back garden. I didn't notice the scenery outside because I was too preoccupied with my own thoughts as I wrapped a hand around the locket. All I saw was the image of Luke before he died, as well as the photograph that had been kept all these years.

I'd been drawn to him like nothing else before, and the more I learnt about Luke, the more I realized that maybe there was truth to his story - I just didn't know how.

"Will you open the box?" From across the room, Sienna inquired. "I've only touched it to bring it downstairs. I'm very curious, and perhaps there are answers inside."

My stomach fluttered with nerves rather than excitement. With a trembling hand, I reached up and rubbed my temples, wishing the throb away while I stared at the mystery box.

It wouldn't open on its own.

I moved to the box with reluctance in every step. I knelt, hesitantly staring at the gift tag once more. I carefully unwound the pink ribbon, folded it, and tucked it into the top of my purse. The gift tag was next. I swallowed hard and quickly removed the lid of the box before backing away. My eyes widened in response to Sienna's gasp. My face was illuminated by a soft glow emanating from within the box. Curiosity overcame my apprehension as I peered inside, revealing a scene that took my breath away.

My bottom hit the floor as the shock of the discovery hit me full force. "It's the dress," I said quietly, my voice cracking slightly. "The one in the photograph." I crept back to the small table, gently pressing my palm against the soft material. The dress had been underrepresented by the black and white, slightly browned, photographic plate. It was powder pink with deeper pink flowers, and the fabric was soft and worn.

I lifted the dress out of the box by the shoulders, gradually unfolding it until the beauty of the dress could be seen. The dress had a small broach at the waist and a matching one further down the dress, until the deep pink flowers grew larger as the dress trailed to the floor. The delicate ruffles cascading down the sleeves added a romantic touch, while the intricate lace detailing along the neckline added a touch of elegance. I ran my fingers over the fabric, imagining myself twirling in the enchanting gown, transporting me to a bygone era of grace and sophistication.

Sienna burst out laughing, jolting me out of the trance. I looked at the other woman, and my eyes widened in surprise as Sienna held out a white cotton chemise with a ruffled neckline and drawers. My surprise turned to amusement when I realized Sienna was holding vintage undergarments.

Sienna draped them over the back of the sofa before pulling out a fine silk corset. "There's also a pair of matching silk shoes and stockings." She leaned close and smoothed her fingers across the silk of the gown. "It's all beautiful."

I nodded gratefully, my fingers lightly tracing the chemise's delicate lace trim. "It's like stepping into a different era," I remarked, my voice tinged with nostalgia.

Sienna smiled, her eyes twinkling with delight. "Luke purchased these for you."

"I need a drink." I sighed. "What are you actually thinking?"

"Aside from thinking about joining you for that drink, only I don't drink, I'm thinking something serious is going on here. I assumed he was insane, but he wasn't, was he? According to what I've heard, Luke hadn't gotten around on his own for years, so everything had to have been planned well before then."

Sienna sat down heavily, the corset she draped over the box, and continued, "I don't know how you could have been there with him in 1912. It has to be one of your relatives, right?"

A long pause followed before I shook my head, agitated. "Neither of us believe that."

"I want to believe because it's logical, but—" Sienna dashed around the coffee table, taking my hands in hers, as she continued, "—what if you were there? What if you traveled back in time?"

I fixed my gaze on Sienna, wanting to believe her. I couldn't comprehend the concept of what she suggested. What Luke suggested.

"Look," Sienna began, "I know I sound crazy, but consider this - Luke knew you. This box has been in his room for years. All you have to do is look at it all to see the facts."

I was as white as the chemise. "The box was gifted with my name, before I was born."

Sienna abruptly snapped. "Did you look for an Esmé Carlisle on the surviving passenger list? What if you were both married?"

I blinked in surprise. "I never gave that a thought." I sighed. "I don't think so because the surnames were alphabetical, and there was only one Carlisle."

"Oh." Sienna fidgeted, attempting to conceal her disappointment.

I wrapped my arm around my midriff and cleared my throat after a few moments of silence. "What do you know about Luke?"

Sienna sighed and shrugged. "Not much, really. I've only been here for about two years to care for Luke. William, his son, has Alzheimer's disease. David, William's son, is rarely seen. But I do know that Luke adopted William after his parents, Olive, and Matthew, died in 1912. They were on the Titanic and never returned home. They'd left William in New York with his grandparents, which was fortunate for him, I suppose."

"I don't know what to say." I cleared my throat, needing to get away and think in my own space. "I'm going to go home for now. I just can't take it all in." I let out a sigh. "I also need to be home before Jake gets there."

"Does Jake realize you no longer want to marry him? If you need a place to live, you could always move in here. I'm sure William wouldn't mind." Sienna shook her head. "I'm staying to help William because, before too long, his Alzheimer's will get worse."

I gave her a wry smile. "I haven't yet told Jake. My thoughts have been preoccupied." I shrugged as I stuffed everything back into the box.

"Will you be all right?" Sienna inquired, concerned.

"I will be." I gathered all of my belongings. "I'll see you tomorrow." I dashed out the door, the box under one arm, before I changed my mind. When I was in Luke's house, I was overcome with raw emotion, which terrified me. Something was going on, and I was convinced that everything I'd learned was true albeit bizarre. Something told me that, however unlikely it seemed, I had been on the RMS Titanic with Luke.

Chapter Five

I was dissatisfied. The locket Luke had given me would not open. And it appeared too fragile to be forced open – I'd considered trying with a knife.

Even staring at the antique didn't help, though I wasn't sure what I expected. It was currently sitting on the coffee table in the apartment I shared with Jake.

The apartment was modern, with the most recent furniture. My favorite feature was the opulent fireplace, which had initially drawn me to the apartment. Although the floor-to-ceiling windows provided a spectacular view of the city, the entire apartment had been decorated around that fireplace.

Jake had chosen the artwork for the walls, and I didn't care for any of it. The throw rugs on the floor in front of the fireplace were my idea, and I loved how much color they added to the apartment.

My gaze returned to the locket just as the doorbell rang. I frowned, unsure who it could be given that I lived a few floors up with concierge and security in the lobby. Jake had insisted on certain requirements.

I noticed the doorman fidgeting in his gray uniform as I peered through the peephole.

Curious, I yanked the door open, only to discover he wasn't alone.

"The courier has a letter for you," he informed me.

"I've been given strict orders to give it to you and no one else on this date. The lawyer was adamant that it couldn't be delivered before or after," the courier admitted as he held out a letter. "You must sign for it. I get a bonus if I can show you received it on this date. So, could you please date your signature?" The courier handed me a clipboard and a pen, and I quickly signed and dated the delivery note.

I felt the color drain from my face as I looked at my name on the envelope. The writing was in the same bold script as the tag on the gift from Luke.

"Thank you," I mumbled as I shut the door behind them.

Jim, the doorman, would be interested in learning about the letter. I was aware that he was a gossip and would be interested in my reaction, but the letter was private.

My legs trembled as I walked slowly into the living room and sat on the sofa. Nervous fingers trembled as they ran over the name on the envelope.

Why would Luke send me a letter that would only be delivered on a specific date? Was it to explain what was going on?

The thought of the words he'd written made me lightheaded. My desire to learn more about Luke ate at me while I was afraid to open the envelope. I debated whether to open it right away or wait, hoping that the passage of time would alleviate my anxiety. As I weighed the options, I wondered if this letter held the key to understanding our relationship or if it would shatter my entire world.

I tore into the envelope and pulled out a cream-colored sheet of paper before I changed my mind.

When I saw the signature at the bottom of the letter, 'Yours forever, Luke', tears welled on my lashes.

"Oh!" I clutched the letter to my chest as tears streamed down my cheeks. I didn't know why I reacted this way, but I needed to put the puzzle pieces together—the pieces that would lead me to Luke Carlisle.

Perhaps the letter would shed light on the situation.

With that thought, I inhaled deeply before exhaling slowly and fully opening the letter.

1987

My dearest Esmé,

You wrote me a letter years ago, which I received after you left. I realized you were telling me the truth after a while. I am not sure how or why you were given to me on the Titanic, but in the short time we were together, I fell completely and hopelessly in love with you.

My life had no meaning after you left. I could not go outside without hoping to spot you amongst the crowds. Every time someone called at the door, I hoped it was you coming home to me. Of course, it never happened, but I never gave up hope that we would be reunited one day.

I have not gone a single day without crying over the beautiful locket you left behind. I miss you with every heartbeat.

I truly believe we will be reunited one day, which is why I need you to believe me and return to me.

We met on the RMS Titanic's promenade on April 10, 1912, as it was being untangled from its near-miss with the New York at Southampton. I remember this day as if it were yesterday, not years ago.

At first sight, my heart leapt from my chest to yours, and you've held it for all these years.

I wish I understood how everything worked, but I do not. All I know is that I have tried everything to bring you back to me.

The clothing I left you in my closet, which I am sure Sienna has discovered by now, as well as the locket, must be worn without any modern clothing. That is all I know.

If everything I have done is not enough for you to come back to me in 1912, and you become a figment of my imagination, please know that I love you with every breath I take.

This letter may appear to be the ramblings of an elderly man, but I assure you that, despite my frailty, I am of sound mind.

I wish I could warn you about how you ended up in 1987, but I am hoping that not saying anything will prevent it from happening again. Maybe I am self-ish, but after all the lonely years I have had, I would like to have you by my side forever.

Our destiny together has not been decided until you return to me in 1912. Everything is subject to change.

Come back to me, Esmé.

Yours forever,

Luke

My face was damp from crying after reading the letter. My heart ached for what Luke must have gone through, and I felt wrecked as a result. It surprised me to realize I wished Luke's fantasies were true. I wished to return to him. I desired to relive the love Luke was convinced we once shared.

I had never had strong feelings for Jake, as painful as it was to admit. Worse, I suspected Jake was having an affair, and the only thing that bothered me about it was that he continued to act as if we were a couple. We were not. Not anymore. Jake was aware of it as well. I felt guilty for leading Jake on, knowing deep down that our relationship had long since lost its luster. I craved the passion and connection I thought Luke could provide, even if it meant confronting the truth about my failing relationship with Jake.

It was late as I gazed out of the window at the dark New York skyline, but what I really saw was the reflection of the demure gown hanging on the closet doors behind me.

I had so many questions, the most pressing of which was, 'How was I on the ship?' Above all, I needed that one question answered. Of course, I wanted to know more about Luke, but it sounded like it all started with the Titanic. Luke had no doubt believed it.

My gaze was drawn to the beautiful dress as I turned to face the closet. I'd never seen anything like it before, and the desire to try it on was getting the best of me. So why not? I had received the dress as a gift, so I had every reason to wear it.

So, what was my hesitation?

Luke's letter had stayed with me since I read it earlier that day. I wondered what he meant about wearing the locket with the clothes he'd left for me. So far, I'd been unable to open the locket.

"I'm not reluctant!" I mumbled with a heavy sigh.

I removed my clothes quickly, and then stepped into the all-in-one chemise and drawers, inhaling, and slowly exhaling as I twirled in front of the mirror, laughing at the sight before me in the vintage undergarments.

It definitely made my heart sing. It was fun to dress up in the pretty clothes. I'd think about everything else later, but I had a dress to put on first. I ignored the corset because it appeared to be torture device.

I stepped carefully into the silk gown, pulling it up my slender limbs, over my hips, and eventually slipping my arms through the delicate cap sleeves. I slipped my feet into the silk stockings and then the shoes, unsurprised that everything fit perfectly. The white stockings felt strange on my legs because they only reached mid-thigh. I disliked anything other than slacks or jeans on my legs.

I turned slowly, surprised to see a regal woman staring back at me. I was slender and medium height, with eyes that sparkled with emotion. My mouth was full, my bone structure delicately carved. The rich auburn hair glistened in the dim light of the room. I was—

"Beautiful," Jake said, surprising me with his presence.

Heat crept onto my cheeks with embarrassment at being caught in the clothing. My fiancé sighed and leaned against the doorjamb. "Why do you have those clothes on?"

I looked over at the box, which had Jake's attention. "It was a gift from someone who died recently."

"The old man?"

The casual way he mentioned Luke irritated me. "His death meant a lot to me. I'd appreciate it if you showed some respect," she said with a hint of temper.

He nodded at my outburst but didn't seem bothered as he lifted the box and tossed it from the bed. Just before the box landed, a loud clunk was heard against the hardwood flooring.

I frowned and went in search of a small silver-haired comb. A poppy detailed the silver before the comb's teeth.

"You are being ridiculous," Jake retorted.

"You just told me I was beautiful." I cocked a brow.

Jake flushed. "You are."

I sighed and walked over to the mirror. "I can't marry you, Jake," I said flatly. I removed the engagement ring and observed his reaction through the mirror. He appeared resigned, as if he'd expected it.

I placed the engagement ring on top of the tallboy before I looked at myself in the mirror. I twisted my long hair up onto the top of my head, admiring myself as I slowly inserted the fancy comb.

As I hung the chain around my neck, I pondered the locket Luke had placed in my hand during our first meeting, as well as the significance of the gift. I went to open the locket.

When I touched the worn clasp, it flipped open. I exclaimed in delight, my surprise visible as I stared at myself and Luke Carlisle. My head began to spin. Buzzing in my ears. My balance was off center. I was falling.

Jake shouted, "Esmé?" His voice sounded distant, as if he were in a tunnel.

"Esmé?" Jake screamed.

I tried to concentrate on his voice, but the room kept spinning, spinning, spinning.

Jake looked at the spot where Esmé had been standing only moments before, and she was gone. *Vanished.* His heart raced, and panic set in. He frantically scanned the room, hoping to catch a glimpse of Esmé, but she was nowhere to be found. Desperation consumed him as he realized she had vanished without a trace. He collapsed onto his knees on the floor. What had happened to her? She'd been looking at the locket, which was open in her hands, and then, *gone. Poof!*

He blinked a few times, wondering how many drinks he'd had before telling Esmé he wanted to end things. She'd gotten there first. When he was reminded, he burst out laughing because, for once, they were on the same page.

But what he'd just witnessed was incomprehensible to him. Was that her way of getting back at him for being in such a bad mood for months? Some trick she'd learned from a magazine or something. It had to be that way. Had it not?

Except he'd seen his ex-fiancée vanish with his own eyes. She'd literally disappeared. As if it were a puff of smoke! As he stood there, stunned, and perplexed, he began to doubt his own sanity. Was this an elaborate illusion, or had he witnessed the impossible? The image of Esmé vanishing haunted him, filling him with dread and an insatiable desire to learn the truth behind her disappearance.

He staggered into the living room, poured himself three fingers of good old Irish whiskey, and sat in his favorite armchair to mull over what to do. He didn't want to remember what had happened in the other room. But he couldn't stop himself. He had witnessed her disappearance with his own eyes. If he told anyone, they'd think he was insane. He would concur with them.

How would he explain where she'd gone? He didn't even know where she'd gone!

Chapter Seven

April 10th, 1912

Noon

AS SOON AS MY HEAD STOPPED SPINNING, I CLOSED my eyes tightly. I listened to the sounds around me: birds squawking, running feet, and distant string instruments. People shouted farewells, and happy cheers continued to make my head throb. I was afraid to open my eyes because everything felt strange to me. My senses were on high alert, so I focused on breathing through the fear, which was when the smell of briny seawater entered my nostrils. A wave of nostalgia washed over me as the scent of seawater brought back memories of my childhood spent by the sea on the California coast. I could almost taste the salt on my lips, as if I was back at the water's edge.

My heart pounded and a sliver of hysteria tried to break through. I quickly turned it off before it took control. *'I love you. Come back to me,'* I told myself over and over in my mind. The silent chant helped me focus.

Minutes must have passed, but I didn't care because something told me I wasn't in New York anymore. I was certain that the world I'd known in 1987 had vanished and that I was no longer a part of it. I just knew it was true. Shivers raced down my spine as I heard the horn of a very large ship blow.

Curiosity gradually overcame the fear, compelling me to finally open my eyes and embrace the strangely familiar world around me. I sat in an Adirondack chair, a rough brown blanket draped over my legs.

My body shook as I swung my feet over the side and stood slowly. I moved closer to the open deck as I needed to peer over the side of the ship. As I gripped the ledge in front of me and peered over the edge, my heart pounded. My gaze trailed down to the dock below, and I realized, astonished, that I was on board the Titanic as it pulled out of Southampton in 1912.

The dock was strewn with people from all walks of life who had gathered to watch the massive ocean liner sail from England on its maiden voyage. I noticed men holding notepads, scribbling words, or drawing pictures that would go down in history. I noticed elegantly dressed women in the crowd, their eyes filled with excitement and anticipation. Some people were waving handkerchiefs as they bid farewell to loved ones who were embarking on this grand adventure. The air was filled with a sense of wonder and possibility, as if everyone present was aware that they were witnessing a moment that would go down in history.

The RMS Titanic would split in two in five days, sink to the ocean floor, and be remembered as one of the greatest maritime disasters. The scene in front of me was a stark contrast to the tragedy that lay ahead, as the ship stood proudly, ready to set sail on its maiden voyage with a sense of invincibility.

I raised my hand and touched the locket. My mind was in turmoil. I'd never imagined anything like this was possible until I awoke on board. Luke had known, so the tidbits of information I'd gleaned about him—and myself—had to be correct. Had we met and fallen in love on this ocean liner before the disaster? If that was the case, how did I end up back in 1987?

I stepped back, looking around, unsure what I was going to do next. I couldn't stand there in an evening gown; other passengers were already staring at me.

Others were dressed casually, while I stood out in the pink gown. It also provided no weather protection, as I shivered when a particularly strong gust of wind whipped through my clothes.

My gaze followed the length of the promenade deck, observing men and women walking by some with children trailing behind them, others with nurse-maids. When they passed by me, they gave me more strange looks, even though they were polite and tipped their heads in greeting. I felt self-conscious as I stood out among the casual wear. I wished I had a coat or a warm sweater to keep the biting wind at bay, but all I had was the flimsy pink gown. Despite the strange looks, I kept my cool and returned the polite greetings with a gracious smile, determined not to let my unusual attire dampen my spirits.

I closed my eyes and pressed my hand to my stomach, trying to shake the unease that had encircled me. I inhaled deeply, opened my emerald-green eyes, and began walking.

I had no idea where I was going or where anything on the ship was, but I knew I had to find Luke and possibly my cabin. That thought brought me stopped me. I'd been in my New York apartment fifteen minutes before, in 1987, and now I was aboard the Titanic in 1912. How could I possibly have a cabin?

The realization that I was time and space displaced overwhelmed me, causing a wave of panic to wash over me. I desperately hoped Luke would have some answers or at the very least provide some sense of familiarity in this perplexing situation.

"I really should have done more research," I grumbled to myself before laughing. When I finally opened the locket around my neck, I hadn't expected to land in 1912. My departure from the future had been swift and unexpected.

"Pardon me, Miss, are you all right?"

I blinked at the crewman who had come to a stop in front of me. He was of medium height, with a wide smile and white teeth in his tanned face.

"I believe I'm turnaround. I have no idea where my cabin is."

Deep in thought, he tipped his head to the side. "Then tell me what number your cabin is, and I'll direct you back."

"I'm afraid I can't remember," I admitted, biting my lip, and feeling sick on the inside for the lie I told. "If I gave you my name, would you mind finding out for me?" I was unsure. "I sincerely apologize. I'm not usually this forgetful, but everything is overwhelming." I swung my arms around, pleading with the young man.

"You stay right here, and I'll go find out. Your name, Miss?"

"Esmé Rogers." The young man smiled and hovered. He drew a rough brown blanket from a deck chair and wrapped it around my shoulders. He spun on his heel and took off at a brisk jog.

I was taken aback by his sudden action, but I smiled anyway. He appeared to be a boy rather than a man, perhaps seventeen—he was gentle.

The blanket was rough, but it kept the chill at bay, which I appreciated as the cold shivers faded.

He came back in no time. "I've found your stateroom." He smiled. "You are really close so let me take you back there. It's on the Promenade Deck." His body language indicated that I should follow him.

"Thank you." I looked around but didn't have time to take anything in because the boy was moving so quickly. Despite his apparent enthusiasm, he probably wanted to keep his distance from me. "I really appreciate it," I said graciously.

"It's no trouble, Miss." He came to a halt and unlocked the cabin door.

"Do you have a key Miss?" He smiled softly.

"I don't think so. I apologize. I must have misplaced it."

"It's no worry, Miss, take this one." He smiled as

he handed over the key he was holding in his open palm.

Did I tip him? With what?

"Oh!" I exclaimed as the door fully opened and the grandeur of the room became apparent. The lower half of the walls were paneled in mahogany, with thick wallpaper covering the top half. A large bed on one side of the room looked so comfortable I wished I could just lie down on top of it. A lovely red and gold sofa was up against the opposite wall, with an armchair nearby. A side table sat beside the chair, and there was a table for two in the center of the room. The room was lit, casting a cozy glow over the elegant furnishings. The ornate chandelier suspended from the ceiling added to the already impressive ambiance.

"It's a lovely stateroom, Miss. The best in the world," the boy said, reminding me that he was standing there.

I blinked and stared at the boy, desiring solitude, but I couldn't let him go without a tip.

Looking around the room, I noticed what appeared to be a purse, so I dashed over and sighed in relief when I discovered some coins. I had no idea what any of it was worth at the time, so I took out one large silver coin, fifty cents, and handed it to the boy.

As he backed out of the room, his eyes glowed.

"Thank you very much, Miss. If you require anything else, please contact John."

I tried to hide my amusement at his excitement over the money. I had clearly given him more than the usual tip. "I will. Thank you once more."

He appeared to be about to say something else before quickly disappearing, the door closing behind him. I sagged into the plush sofa, which wasn't as comfortable as I'd hoped.

12:30

My gaze wandered around the room as I attempted to explain why my name was on a stateroom and why there were items in the room. I had accomplished the impossible by traveling through time.

Whoever I was in 1912, I obviously had money. The stateroom had to have cost a fortune. Nothing had been overlooked in the room's elegance, and apart from the gentle rolling of the liner, the silence was soothing.

I moved forward slowly, letting the blanket fall from my shoulders to the sofa. A door to the left of the room drew my attention, but when I placed my hand on the cold, smooth steel handle, it remained stationary. Locked.

Maybe a connecting room?

The other door in the room led to a dressing area brimming with clothes, shoes, and accessories. I noticed some more corsets among the items, which I would never consider wearing. To my relief, the dresses were divided into day and evening wear. The shoes appeared to be arranged in rows, beginning with the palest pink and gradually deepening in color. I admired the shoes' meticulous organization, each pair perfectly aligned. The accessories, on the other hand, were a jumbled mess of jewelry, hats, and handbags that added a sense of whimsy and individuality to the look.

The small door to the side led to a water closet with a cluttered vanity. I moved over and picked up a small pot of what I assumed was moisturizer, curious about what women used at the time. There were two small pots, both in gold. One contained bright red powder, while the other contained pale pink powder. In a small green container sat a small pot of poudre de riz. I smiled, overjoyed with my find, especially since it was the same one that I used to set my make-up in 1987. The packaging was different. When I opened the last pot, I found black sludge. "I've no idea how to what you are," I muttered to the pot as I tightened the lid.

My gaze was drawn to the regal mirror, and for the first time since opening my eyes on board the ship, I felt as if I could breathe. My stomach was still knotted, but the fact that I looked the same, if a little befuddled, helped to calm my nerves. I noticed a glimmer of familiarity in my eyes as I examined my reflection, a hint of the adventurous spirit that had led me to embark on this time-traveling adventure. I decided to embrace the unknown and make the most of my unexpected trip back in time with a newfound sense of determination.

What would my next move be? Would Luke recognize me? What would I tell him? Should I try to warn the captain of what was going to happen? He'd probably think I was insane. Who wouldn't?

I returned to the main room, unsure where to begin. Perhaps by changing into a daytime outfit? As I turned slightly, the door to the room began to open, and I remained frozen as a teenage girl appeared in the doorway. She was dressed in a maid's uniform.

"Oh!" exclaimed the girl, reaching for her chest. "I've been looking all over for you."

"You have?" I responded, surprised. "Um, I forgot where the stateroom was."

The girl moved closer as she closed the door

behind her. "I take it you really like that dress if you're wearing it now?"

"Um," I said before looking up to meet the girl's gaze, "I love this dress, but I think I should change."

"That would be a good idea." The young lady laughed.

Surprised, I let the young girl fuss over me and watched as she chose a cream day dress from the selection in the closet. The skirt was covered in tiny peach flowers, and the top was plain cream with fine lace. It was lovely, but I had no idea who this girl was and had no idea how to ask when we clearly knew each other.

"You'll look so pretty in this," sighed the girl.

"It really is a lovely dress, um, um—" I waved my arms.

"Violet. I'm eighteen, Miss," the young girl said, a frown on her face.

I tapped my brow. "I apologize. I must have gotten colder outside than I thought, and your name slipped my mind."

Violet burst out laughing. "Oh, don't be concerned, Miss. After all, we only met a little more than an hour ago, before you boarded the ship. I was hired by your parents' lawyer. God bless them."

"That's right," I murmured, swallowing hard.

Violet started undoing my dress, and when I stepped out of it, the girl gasped. "Your corset has disappeared."

I laughed at the shock on Violet's face. My gaze wandered to the closet and the other agonizing corsets.

"You must wear one, Miss. What will others think?"

Another giggle escaped my lips. "Unless I get undressed in front of them, I don't see how they will know I'm not wearing one."

"But everyone wears them. You must as well." Violet dashed to the closet and yanked one off the hanger.

When Violet confronted me with the torturous contraption in her hands, I shook my head. "I'm sorry, Violet, but I'm not wearing that corset or any other. I wish to breathe, but I won't be able to in that thing."

Amused at the shock on Violet's face, I turned and twirled in my undergarments. "Let's get me into the dress so we can go and explore."

"You," Violet paused, "want me to explore the ship with you?"

"Of course, I do!" I scowled. "You're the only friend I have on this ship." I wondered whether those words were true the moment I said them.

"I suppose I could hold your jacket or something. We could observe what is happening in the water. The Titanic drew the New York toward us, and we narrowly avoided colliding," Violet explained while I pulled on the lovely day gown.

I only just caught sight of Violet as her hand reached for my neck, my thoughts having been elsewhere. I quickly ducked out of the way and coughed. "I wear this necklace always." I ran my fingers over the delicate jewelry. "I can't explain, but never remove it." I smiled to soften the sting of my words.

I found having a maid strange. I'd had to do everything myself my entire adult life. With that in mind, I turned to Violet. "I have an idea." I grabbed the girl's arm and dragged her into the closet.

"Let me take a look. We have similar build, though you are slightly shorter than I." I went through the clothes and found a peach day dress. It was white with embroidered flowers on the skirt and sleeves. "This is very you."

I turned to face the pale Violet who whispered in confusion, "I don't understand, Miss."

I shook my head and pushed the dress into Violet's arms. "I'll wait in the bedroom while you change into this."

"What? No way, Miss! I'm not allowed to wear your clothes. They'd throw me overboard."

"Nonsense! They would not throw anyone overboard. Do you have passage on the ship?"

Violet gave a nod.

"This is my idea, now please hurry and put the dress on so that you may accompany me to lunch, followed by a stroll down the promenade in the fresh air?"

I didn't wait for Violet to decide, I simply closed the door with the girl on the other side.

I couldn't remember the last time I had so much fun.

14:40

Even with the thicker day dress on, the promenade deck was freezing in the brisk weather. Violet had reminded me of this, which I appreciated. I smiled as I looked at Violet, who appeared befuddled and doe-eyed, but still very pretty. Her young face was framed by wisps of dark brown hair.

Violet's cheeks were flushed from the cold, giving her skin a rosy glow, which I noticed. Despite her discomfort, I admired Violet's fortitude and ability to maintain her poise in such frigid conditions.

Violet was going to be a great friend, I was certain. If I could only get her to act like she belonged in the clothes she wore. I wasn't the best person to teach someone proper etiquette, but we could have fun trying.

"Violet, you need to walk beside me with your head held high." I followed my own advice. Violet looked at me out of the corner of her eye, ready to flee to the safety of the room. "Be confident, even if you're sick with nerves and fright. Don't let anyone see how you truly feel."

Violet lifted her head slowly, and I smiled to encourage. "Don't look at your feet again." I chuckled.

I missed a step forward when I noticed the man walking toward us in a lighthearted conversation with another man who was holding a beautiful woman on his arm.

The man with the couple was tall, dark, and handsome, and just looking at him made my heart skip a beat. His broad shoulders filled his jacket, and I couldn't take my gaze away even when I felt a tug on my sleeve.

Luke.

Violet hissed, "Miss, Miss." She tugged on my sleeve again, hoping to get me to move.

"I can't move," I said quietly.

Just as the three newcomers were about to pass, the man I couldn't take my gaze from turned his head and met my gaze. His gaze had a moment of recognition, as if he had seen me before. My heart skipped a beat, and I felt a rush of heat rush through my body. The man's lips curled into a small smile.

His speech stopped abruptly, and he stood still, even as the man and woman continued walking.

Matthew and Olive?

"Luke, do you know this lady?" the man nudged Luke.

I snapped out of the trance and found Luke doing the same. He cleared his throat and extended his hand, "Luke Carlisle," while maintaining his gaze on mine.

"Esmé Rogers," I exhaled, my heart racing. My trembling fingers touched the warmth of Luke's extended hand. My palm slid softly against Luke's, and when he encircled my hand possessively, I hoped he would never let me go.

The other man swallowed and cleared his throat. "Luke, where are your manners?" He frowned and shifted his gaze between myself and Luke.

Luke blinked a few times before slowly releasing my hand. He kept me close to his side by placing a protective hand on the small of my back.

Violet remained off to one side as the man and woman continued to give us odd glances. Luke adjusted his grip and reached for my elbow. His fingers sensually stroked the tender underside of my arm.

"Esmé——" he said, as if he'd just taken a bite of the finest chocolate "—let me introduce you to my brother, Matthew, and his wife, Olive."

My heart sank because I knew they wouldn't be alive in five days. On the tip of my tongue was the desire to warn them to leave the ship in France, for all of them to leave in France. After a brief pause, I added, "It's nice to meet you both." Was it me who moved closer to Luke, or was it Luke who moved closer to me? I couldn't decide. "Let me introduce you to my close friend, Violet." Her voice trailed off as I met Luke's gaze once more.

"Violet Gibson." When Violet spoke up, I let out a relieved laugh.

"I'm sorry, my mind has momentarily deserted me," I apologized, a blush spreading across my face.

Matthew burst out laughing. "You're not the only one who is having trouble remembering their manners today." He fixed his gaze on his brother, who blushed. "Perhaps, you both would like to join us at our table tonight for dinner?" Gentle lines of laughter framed Matthew's mouth and creased the sides of his dark eyes. He was a shadowy figure, large and powerful, and nearly as tall as Luke.

I raised my gaze to Luke, who waited for their answer.

"We would love to. Thank you for inviting us," I replied.

"Luke, we have business to finish discussing," Matthew reminded him.

"It's been my pleasure to meet you both," Olive said. "I look forward to not being the only woman at the table this evening." Her bluish-green eyes sparkled with excitement as she smiled brightly. She appeared more delicate and ethereal than anyone I had ever met before, and she exuded gentleness. As they stood and talked, her lovely caramel brown curls were windblown.

Luke made a possessive motion with his arm up to my shoulder before reluctantly letting go. "This evening," he explained. "I'm not going to be able to concentrate on business now that I've met you," he said quietly to me.

My fingers flew to my neck, where my pulse pounded. "I look forward to seeing you again."

Matthew cleared his throat, but this time he grabbed Luke's elbow and yanked him along with them.

Luke's gaze remained fixed on me until we vanished inside. Violet raised her brow and moved to stand in front of me. "What was it you said earlier about letting people see how you really feel? Or did I get that lesson wrong?" she joked.

I opened my mouth to respond before snapping it shut. I suppressed my laughter as I realized how amusing the whole situation was. "I take that back, but only if you meet the most handsome man."

"He is handsome, and he certainly found you pleasant." Violet smiled briefly before frowning. "I've never seen two people meet quite like that before. Are you certain you've never met him?"

"I am certain." To all intents and purposes, we hadn't met before because Luke had aged since our first meeting in 1987. "I think I need a nap."

"Me too. It's exhausting being your friend," Violet grumbled, giggling as she did so. "The truth is I am having more fun than I've ever had before."

"I'm glad." As we moved along, I slid my arm through Violet's.

We turned quickly as footsteps thundered down the promenade. Luke rushed through the door, looking a little disheveled.

He took two powerful strides toward me, while Violet slipped away. He pushed stray hairs away from my cheeks, and I leaned lightly into him as he tilted my chin up.

His large hands tenderly cupped my face. "I've never been so open with a woman in my life, but there's something about you. I need to feel you to make sure you're real. I'm not sure what's going on with me." He burst out laughing. "I'm not making sense, but just this once, for a moment in time, I need to do this in order to take my next breath." As he spoke, his lips brushed lightly against mine before claiming my mouth in a surprisingly gentle kiss.

I couldn't stop thinking about Luke as he caressed my soft lips with his own. My hands trembled as I reached up, around to the nape of his neck.

Luke raised his mouth from mine and looked into my eyes, letting me see everything I'd made him feel.

"We were meant to be together," I said quietly.

Luke swallowed and took a step back, his breathing hard. "This evening," he said as if it were a proclamation.

"Yes."

He vanished as quickly as he appeared.

"You could at least play hard to get," Violet said, a smile on her lips.

A soft smile slid across my lips as I covered my

mouth with trembling fingers. I smile at my friend. "He's my soul mate, Violet."

18:30

Even with my thicker day dress on, the promenade deck was freezing in the brisk weather. Violet had reminded me of this, which I appreciated. My smile was fixed, and it made me happy to watch Violet, who appeared befuddled and doe-eyed, but still very pretty. Wisps of dark brown hair framed her young face. I stood on deck next to Violet, the young girl giddy with delight at seeing Cherbourg, France. All I could see was the way Luke had locked his gaze on mine just before kissing me. The taste of him was still lingering on my tongue. It had been so unexpected. On such a brief acquaintance, he was rather brazen. I smiled softly as I lifted my hand to my lips in remembrance.

"Are you going to be hard to get tonight, Miss?" Violet inquired, her eyes twinkling with delight.

I burst out laughing. "I have no intention of being *hard* to get. The man has me, and I believe he knows it."

Violet let out a loud sigh. "They do say this is the ship of dreams, so I guess dreams do come true."

I turned to face the young girl, my voice wishing

her well. "Sometimes, dreams are all that people have. Violet, never give up on them."

"None of my dreams have ever come true."

"Tell me what you'd want if you believed in dreams," I inquired, moving in closer.

Violet's eyes glazed over for several minutes before she turned her entire body toward me. Her eyes glowed with delight. "My wish would be to stay in New York and make something of myself," she said, gesticulating with her hands. "I'd like to make ladies' dresses, but not just any old dresses. Create design them."

"Then dream, Violet."

Her brow furrowed. "I won't be allowed to stay in New York."

I frowned and tilted Violet's face up so that our eyes met. "What exactly do you mean? I thought you were my employee?"

"Yes, Miss. But I've been engaged by a family from New York who is sailing on the Titanic."

"Hmm," I muttered, smiling. "We'll see," I said, feeling the color drain from my face the moment the words left my mouth. Did Violet she survive the sinking?

"Miss, you've gone white."

I gasped for air. "Please refer to me as Esmé from

now on. After all, we're friends now." I smoothed my hands slowly along the pink dress and over my hips. "I'm fine," I assured Violet, who did not appear convinced.

"I just know something," I said, forcing a smile as I fidgeted with the bracelet around my wrist. "I don't know how to tell what I know or even if I should tell."

What if I told the captain and he actually listened to me without dismissing me as insane? Would it alter history? Would that mean I stayed in 1912 with Luke, or would I end up back in 1987 with Luke pleading for my return?

My head hurt from all of it. Despite what I'd seen in movies, no one had ever been able to time travel, as far as I knew. But I was in 1912, so anything was possible. I would delegate the science to someone else.

The bugler's rendition of 'The Roast Beef of Old England' interrupted my thoughts. He was informing the passengers that dinner was on its way.

My stomach fluttered with nervousness. "It's time."

I grinned. Violet looked stunning in the evening gown she had been hesitant to wear.

We made our way through the ship, nervously, toward the dining saloon.

I took a deep breath as I reached the top of the

grand staircase. I'd only seen black and white photographs of the masterpiece while watching a documentary. The shipwreck was discovered in 1985, and reports stated that the staircase did not survive the sinking.

Standing here, looking down, gave me a strange sensation, one that made my head spin. I was thankful to have Violet with me because the girl had once again helped to bring me back to the present and settle me.

Reaching out, I placed a hand on the banister and began to descend, Violet close behind. Violet appeared to be bursting at the seams with excitement. That was the feeling I had when I turned to go into the saloon and saw Luke standing off to the side.

As everyone else faded into the background, my breath caught in the back of my throat. All I saw was Luke moving toward me in his dinner suit, his gaze never leaving mine.

"Esmé," he exhaled the words. "I've been expecting you. His fingers slid sensuously over the skin of my arm where my long, white gloves ended, his gaze falling to my red lips.

I blurted out, "I'm afraid."

Luke frowned and placed a finger on my trembling lips. "You don't have to be afraid of me. I'll never hurt you."

"No, I'm afraid I'll hurt you," I admitted, tears falling from my lashes. "I don't want to hurt you."

He kept his gaze fixed on me. "Let me worry about myself," he said as he extended his arm to me. "I'd like to accompany, Violet, and yourself into dinner."

Moments passed, and butterflies flew in my stomach as I slipped my hand through his arm and grabbed his forearm, his muscles tensing under my gentle touch.

He cleared his throat and smiled encouragingly at Violet. She smiled and gently slipped her arm through his.

"I'm a lucky man tonight, having two beautiful ladies escort me into dinner." He smiled at Violet, who beamed up at him, and then turned his gaze to me.

I felt as if I'd known him my entire life when he looked at me, and his gaze seemed to sink into my senses. Despite the fact that we had only recently met, I knew I would do anything to remain in 1912 and spend the rest of my life with Luke Carlisle.

I smiled lovingly at him and watched as his eyes danced with delight before we were interrupted.

"May I photograph you?" enquired a small man, looking to weigh significantly less than the heavy equipment he carried over his shoulder. "It won't take but a moment."

Violet quickly backed away as Luke carefully positioned us. It took a few moments to take the photograph. When Luke began to lead me away, I noticed RMS Titanic printed on the glass of the door we had stood beside.

The glass-plated photograph.

My eyes were sad, and my stomach fluttered with unease.

"Is everything okay?" Luke inquired, concerned.

I smiled as I turned to face Luke. "I think it is," I said, and with Luke looking at me the way he was, I was more than certain everything was fine.

He gently squeezed my arm before reaching for Violet, who had reappeared.

As we moved through the elegant dining saloon, I felt my equilibrium return in my beautiful surroundings. The floor had a red and gold pattern, and the walls had white Jacobite wooden paneling. Leaded-glass windows were lit from behind to conceal the portholes.

Matthew greeted us at our table, while Luke seated Violet next to a young man he introduced as James Calder. James was a tall, attractive man with lines around his mouth and eyes from laughter. His black hair was cut short, but it appeared to be unruly if not tamed. His gunmetal gray eyes were fixed on Violet, who was flushed on the cheeks.

As Luke sat me beside him, I returned Olive's knowing smile. Luke sat beside me, his arm brushing mine. I relished the heat from his body and, daringly, moved my thigh so that it pressed against his.

When his brother cleared his throat, his large neck trembled. "I hope you got some good rest this afternoon?" Matthew enquired. "Olive insisted on investigating her surroundings."

"Thank you. We did." I smiled at Olive. "We intend to spend more time exploring the ship tomorrow. Also, Violet and I are both excited for our morning arrival in Queenstown, where we should have a beautiful view of Ireland's coast."

"We've never been to Ireland," Olive said, smiling. "Because Matthew had business in London, we left our young child in New York. It was far less difficult than bringing him with a nanny. Besides, he's safer back home."

Matthew burst out laughing. "I keep telling Olive that we're on an unsinkable ship," he said as he affectionately patted her hand. "We'll be home soon with our son. We've missed him terribly."

"I've missed having him to spoil," Luke said with a wide smile.

"How old is he?" I asked.

"William is a cheeky two-year-old," Olive explained. "Do you have any relatives in America, Esmé?"

Luke fiddled with a hair tendril at the nape of my neck, and his touch sent goose bumps down my spine, making concentrating on conversation, and *breathing* difficult.

I looked at him, unable to take my gaze away from his hypnotic gaze as he offered me a lazy smile.

"Um—" I stuttered, giving my attention to the other occupants of the table. "Family? I don't have family in New York, but I do have distant relatives in Boston," I said. "My parents died, so I'm going to New York," I said, smiling and looking at Violet, who was blushing at James' attention. "I'm accompanied by my good friend Violet. We'll be having new adventures."

"Hopefully not alone," Luke quietly added.

I fixed my gaze on him. "If that is an invitation for you to show us around New York, then I gladly accept."

He smiled. "It most certainly was an invitation."

"Perhaps I could invite myself," James said, his gaze still fixed on Violet, who appeared smitten.

Violet remained silent, so I spoke for her. "We'd love to have you join us, Mr. Calder. Violet, wouldn't we?" I reached out with my foot over Luke's leg and gently kicked the other woman to get her attention.

Luke erupted into laughter. "I think she's in agreement," he remarked, laughing.

Dinner began to be served, and I was too preoccupied with Luke's proximity to pay attention to what I ate. Every glance, every slight touch heightened my awareness of the man.

When the meal was finished, the orchestra began to play, and Luke extended his hand to me as he pushed away from the table. "Please dance with me, Esmé."

"Where?" I asked quietly.

He smiled as he said, "There's a small, open space."

I reached out, my fingers intertwining with his, and let him lead me to the dance floor. His arm slipped around my waist, and he affectionately brushed a kiss to my cheek. "I've wanted you in my arms since the first time we met. It's hard to believe it was just a few hours ago. It feels a far longer."

"I agree." Overwhelmed with emotion, I dropped my forehead to his chest and felt him kiss the top of my head.

"Look at me, Esmé," he instructed. "Please allow me to see your lovely face. It makes my heart pound so see how you look at me because no one has ever looked at me the way you do. As if I'm the only one they see, want, or require."

"You are all I see," I leaned in close to him, our lips a breath apart, "and I want you. I want so much to be with you, and it's scary because we've only just met."

"It is scary, but now I've found you, I'm not prepared to let you go."

"You might not like me when we get to know each other."

Luke pressed me up against his tense body. "That will never happen," he firmly stated. "Never, Esmé."

Before he lifted his gaze to mine, his eyes burned as they focused on my lips. "Do you believe me?"

"Yes," I said, moving away from him slightly. Luke needed to cool down because the heat was getting to me.

He stopped dancing and said, "I need some fresh air. Would you like to walk with me?"

As he escorted me from the dining saloon to the promenade, I enjoyed the feel of his hand on the small of my back.

Luke laughed and said, "I can breathe again. I always feel like everyone is watching me," he smirked. "I'm delighted to have met you. You made it tolerable."

"You being with me makes everything that's

happened to get here bearable," I admitted, my fingers cold against his cheeks. "I'm so afraid that we'll have everything, and then it will all be taken away from us."

Luke frowned, his gaze caressing my face. "Why do I have the impression you know something?"

"These sudden and intense feelings I have for you frighten me," I explained, not yet telling him the truth. There would be another opportunity to tell him the truth, and hopefully he wouldn't think I was insane.

I reached out and lightly pressed my hand against his chest, sighing when he pressed his palm against my hip. His free hand carelessly moved to my neck, softly holding me as his thumb caressed over my pulse. "You're unique, Esmé Rogers," he said softly against my lips.

As we leant closer, chatter from behind Luke pushed us apart slightly. As he watched me shiver in the cold night, Luke removed his dinner jacket, wrapping it around my shoulders and keeping his arm around me.

I leaned in against him, my face against his chest. "Tell me about Luke Carlisle and why he was in London on business."

He laughed softly. "Our father founded an engineering firm England. Not far from London. It turned out that one of the parts our father began making is required inside an automobile's engine. It cannot function without it."

"That's absolutely amazing," I said, tilting my head to Luke's, wondering why I hadn't realized that before.

"It can be inconvenient and messy," he admitted, smiling. "But it's a very profitable business, so I have no complaints," he said softly. "If I hadn't been on business then I never would have met you."

He leaned down and curled his fingers into the back of my hair.

As his mouth descended, I felt my knees weaken. "I'm going to kiss you right now." His last words were smothered by our lips, and we were both surprised by my eager response to the touch of his lips.

As he roused my passion, I pushed my fingers through his thick, black hair, while his grip tightened.

Shivers of pleasure accompanied each touch as his kiss became more urgent and exploratory before he left a trail of fire along my jaw and grazed my earlobe with his warm mouth.

"I need to take you to your cabin," he said under his breath, "and leave you safely behind the door until I collect you for breakfast."

"Mmm, I like the breakfast idea," I mumbled,

while craving, aching for another kiss from his swollen lips.

Luke sighed and moved me away from him, his hands resting on my shoulders. My hands caressed his chest, and when he took a deep breath, I snatched them back, wrapping them around my stomach. I wanted this man more than my next breath and that scared the very life out of me.

"Can you tell me where your cabin is?" He asked.

"Close."

He sighed. "So is mine," he admitted with a chuckle. "You've been sent to torture me."

Luke wrapped his arm around my shoulders as I led the way inside. "This one is mine," Luke said as we approached my cabin, "just so you know where to find me if you need anything."

He was startled by my surprised laugh, so I explained, "I think we have adjoining rooms."

"What?" His eyes widened before he closed them and inhaled deeply. "Please keep your side locked at all times. I honestly don't trust myself to be alone in a private room with you." He gulped. "I'll knock at eight for breakfast."

He quickly moved away after kissing me on the cheek. I heard his door open and close a few moments later.

My huge grin remained as I dashed into my cabin, where I ran and dived onto the bed, rolling to my back.

"I love you, Luke Carlisle," I said quietly, my hand covering my mouth to keep the excited giggle at bay.

I was ecstatic and couldn't wait to see him in the morning. My gaze was drawn to the locked door that separated our staterooms. I'd never been more tempted to open a door.

I refused.

My eyes began to close as I wondered what Jake and Sienna thought of my disappearance back in 1987.

SIENNA NEARLY JUMPED OUT OF HER SKIN WHEN THE doorbell chimed. It was loud and unexpected. From her position at the dining room table, she couldn't make out who it was. She placed her pen down beside her notebook. As she approached the front door, Sienna's heart raced with anticipation. She hoped it was someone she knew and not a stranger.

"Who is it?" she shouted through the door.

"Um, Jake Preston. I'm looking for a Sienna Taylor. She was a friend of my fiancée, Esmé Rogers."

Her heart raced because she'd wondered what had happened to her new friend. She hadn't been able to get in touch with Esmé since she'd left with the box of clothing.

"Is everything all right with her?"

"No," he moaned. "She's disappeared and I wondered if you knew where she was. I mean," he laughed, "one minute she was in front of me and the next she wasn't. I know I sound crazy, but I need to talk."

The minute she heard about Esmé, she panicked and quickly unfastened the locks. When she heaved the heavy door open, she was startled to find Jake Preston looking less than immaculate. When she'd seen him in the restaurant the night, she had first met Esmé, he'd been neat as a pin, now he wore scruffy jeans, a sweater with a hole in the sleeve and a head of disheveled hair. The thought that she preferred him this way popped into her head, which she shook away. No way would she think of her friend's fiancé in that way.

"I'm Sienna." She stepped away from the door. "I think you better come in."

"Thank you." He sighed in relief and hovered while she closed the front door.

"I have a pot of coffee in the dining room if you'd like a cup?" Sienna offered, leading him through to where she'd been sitting, pondering.

"I wouldn't say no." Jake smiled, taking the offered seat.

Sienna joined him after she'd topped her own cup up with the steaming liquid. They sat together in silence for a long time, until Jake started talking.

"We'd been arguing, and she'd just put an end to our engagement." He sighed. "I'd actually been out drinking, trying to work up the courage to do the same. I think Esmé thought I was having an affair." He laughed. "I'm not a man who would ever be unfaithful, no matter how unhappy I was. I just figured it was easier letting her think that. Maybe she'd end our engagement quicker. She never did because I don't think she cared enough about me to be bothered." He shrugged.

Sienna kept quiet. She'd gotten the same impression from Esmé, so he was on the right track, but he didn't need her confirming it.

"That night, I came home, and she had on an old dress. I flung the box it had obviously come into the floor and out flew a hair comb." He swallowed and held her gaze. "She put the comb in her hair, and then fastened the necklace around her neck. The one with the locket that wouldn't open."

Leaning forward in his chair, and in a controlled voice, he continued, "She vanished. She had no trouble opening the locket. She gasped when she took a closer look, and then that part of the bedroom, where she stood, went hazy. When it cleared, she was *gone*." Jake threw his hands in the air. "Vanished into thin air, without a trace," he exclaimed, frustration evident in his voice. "I searched the entire room, but there was no sign of her."

"Where did she go?" Sienna asked, more to herself than Jake.

"I don't know, which is why I'm here. The doorman gave me your message to her, a couple of days ago. So here I am."

"I don't know what to think." Sienna felt all the blood rushing around in her head because, surely, Esmé hadn't discovered a way to go back to Luke?

"You know something. I can see it on your face." Jake watched her carefully.

"What I know will sound as crazy as you do about her just disappearing."

"After what I saw, I'll believe anything. Trust me on that." Jake's eyes begged.

Sienna nodded, and admitted, "Luke was a survivor of the Titanic. He never spoke about it to me or anyone as far as his son, William, knows. Luke, apparently, became a recluse not long after he arrived back in New York on board the Carpathia. William said there was speculation that he'd met a woman on board and fell in love with her. The conclusion was that she'd drowned, but, more recently—"

"Sienna, do you have my reading glasses?" William interrupted as he walked into the room. He glanced up from the paper in his weathered hand. "Oh! I didn't know you had a visitor. My apologies." He was a slim man with neatly trimmed snow-white hair.

"It's okay, William. Come and meet Esmé's—"

"Friend," Jake finished.

"Esmé?" William asked, confused.

"She held your father's hand when he died. You met her afterward and at the funeral," Sienna reminded. "You'd been out at the club when she was here asking about a photograph your father gave her."

"Ah!" He tapped his forehead and stared at Jake. "This isn't as good as it once was." He shook his head, a frown darkening his features. "Esmé," he mumbled to himself. "I know that name." He joined them at the table.

Sienna passed him his glasses, which he ignored, lost in thought. She turned back to Jake, and whispered, "I'm sorry. He forgets things."

Jake smiled. "It's okay. Do you mind continuing?"

"I can do that." She glanced at William and back to Jake. "Before Luke died, he told Esmé he loved her. He told her to 'come back to me'. He left clues and things for her, and we were even starting to believe it was possible."

"Esmé!" William burst out, smacking his palm on the table, grinning. "I thought my memory was failing me again."

"I don't understand." Sienna watched him.

"Esmé was the name of the woman my father was in love with."

Unable to form any words, Sienna stared at him.

He continued, "Both of you come with me."

If it hadn't been for Jake, she'd have stayed in the dining room, but he pulled her out of the chair and kept his hand on her arm as they followed the old man through the house and into an office.

"He told me about Esmé when I found a small box buried in one of his drawers. It contained a locket. He was so angry I'd stumbled upon it. But then he told me he'd fallen madly in love with Esmé, a woman he'd met onboard the titanic. When he talked about her, it was the first time I'd ever seen my father cry. It broke my heart to see how distressed he was over her loss. I'd actually forgotten, until last week." He laughed. "I can't remember what I did yesterday, but I remem- bered that from when I must have been around five- years-old." He shook his head sadly.

Jake pulled Sienna down to the sofa with him, just

as her legs were about to give way. They both watched as William flicked through a large box of papers.

"What are you looking for?" Jake asked.

The older man froze. "This." He pulled out a large, square photograph. "I found this last week, which jogged my memory."

He held it out, and Jake took it. Sienna was too shaky to even think straight, let alone hold something so delicate.

Jake turned it so they could both look at it and sucked in a harsh breath when he saw his ex-fiancée staring back at him.

"The inscription on the back says Luke Carlisle and Esmé Rogers. It's also dated."

Jake flipped the photograph.

April 13th, 1912.

"It was taken on the outside deck of the Titanic." Sienna frowned. "How did it survive?"

Jake flipped it back over. "It's been folded at one time. See?" Jake trailed his finger along what looked to be crease marks. "I think he may have had this restored. I don't understand how this is even possible. That's Esmé." Jake laughed. "Although, I never thought it was possible for someone to just vanish either."

"But this is proof she made it back to him, Jake."

"Why would she go back to him if she knows she'll die a few days later? That doesn't make sense."

"Now I'm confused so I'll leave you both to get on with it." William disappeared, closing the door on his way out.

"Maybe," Sienna answered Jake, "she thought she could change history." She shrugged.

"Or maybe she thought it was the easiest way to leave me," Jake offered.

Sienna, blinked. "Don't think that way." She placed a hand on his arm. "Esmé has been obsessed with Luke and finding answers from the moment she met him. She said he was familiar to her, but yet she had no memory of why."

He sighed heavily. "So, what do we do now?"

"I honestly don't know."

Chapter Nine

April 11th, 1912

11:20

LUKE WATCHED ME ACROSS THE CARD TABLE AS I tried my best to concentrate on the game of bridge. It was the only game I knew how to play and the only one that Violet, Luke and James knew how to play. I wasn't doing very well because I was too distracted by the handsome man who wouldn't stop looking at me. He had me upside down and swimming in an assortment of nerves.

"I think we should take a walk along the promenade soon so you can see Ireland when we get to Queenstown, which I think you said you wanted to see," Luke suggested.

"I'd love to." I turned to Violet and raised my eyebrows. The girl blushed. "I'm sure James wouldn't mind joining us."

James laughed. "I'd love to." He pushed away from the table. "I think we should forget about the cards, since I don't think anyone's really interested. Let's take the walk now." He held out his arm to Violet, who looked equally excited.

"Alone at last," Luke commented, pulling his chair closer. "I've been waiting for this moment since you left your room this morning." His fingers brushed my cheek as he leaned forward and brushed a soft kiss on my lips. "So precious."

I slipped a hand to my stomach, holding on tightly so I wouldn't reach for him. From the look in his eyes, he knew exactly what I wanted. "Are you going to behave yourself today?" he whispered.

"In public, I will," I teased.

Luke paused for a moment before throwing his head back and laughing. A few heads turned in our direction, but we ignored them.

"I think you are going to be trouble in more ways than one," he admitted, getting to his feet. "Shall we?"

I took his offered arm and allowed him to lead me to the promenade. "I hope Olive is feeling better. I missed her at breakfast."

With a smile in his eyes, he leaned close. "Between you and me, I think she's pregnant," he grinned. "I love babies! What about you?"

"I haven't thought about children, but I think I'd like some."

"Hmm," Luke laughed. "How many is some?"

I grinned, watching him out of the corner of my eye. "I thought ten would be nice number."

He coughed and stuttered. "Ten?"

Laughing, I added, "One or two would be fine." I patted his arm. "I take it you want to be the father?" My lips twitched as I met his serious gaze. The smile slowly faded from my face.

"Yes." Luke's one word made my head spin as he urged me to keep walking. "And don't think I haven't noticed that you always change the subject to me when I ask you something personal."

I knew he was going to notice something so obvious; I just didn't know what to say. So, I gave him something. "I'm originally from Boston. My father was a banker before he and my mother were killed in an accident." It was all true. "I'll tell you everything soon, although I'm afraid you'll think I'm crazy."

His hand cupped my jaw and tilted my face up to his. He looked into my eyes and then placed a soft kiss on my lips. "I promise I won't think you're crazy." He quickly kissed me again before pulling me over to the side of the ship. "Ireland."

I gasped, a smile forming on my lips. "I've always wanted to visit Ireland, so to actually see it fills me with excitement."

"I'll bring you back one day," Luke whispered in my ear, his arm holding me close.

My happiness faded at the thought of one day. Would I still be with Luke, or would I somehow end up back in my time?

"Did I scare you?" Luke asked, sensing my distress.

Reaching for his hand at my waist, I intertwined my fingers with his and then reassured him, "Talking about a future with a man I've only just met should scare me, but I find it does not. It makes me impatient," I turned my face to his, "to have that future.

Luke groaned and closed his eyes as he caught his breath. "Please look at Ireland," he moaned and opened his eyes. "If you keep looking at me like that, I'm going to embarrass us both."

I stepped between him and the side of the ship. I looked out as we anchored about two miles off Queenstown, known in 1987 as Cobh.

Feeling unsteady, I took his hands in mine and wrapped his arms around me, our fingers intertwined and held the connection between us.

We stood for a long time, watching the small boats and ferries making their way to the ship. Neither of us said anything, neither of us wanted to break the silence of the loving and caring embrace we shared.

It wasn't until the passengers actually started to come aboard from the tender ferries that Luke moved me away from the side of the ship. "I could hold you in my arms all day, but maybe you'd like a cup of tea to warm you up?"

"That would be lovely." I felt robbed when Luke dropped his hands from around my waist. I smiled broadly as he cupped my elbow to lead me away from the promenade.

As soon as we entered the lounge, Olive and Matthew waved us over. "Please join us," Olive invited, sitting on one of the couches in the spacious area. It reminded me of a hotel lobby, only more extravagant and lavishly decorated like the Palace of Versailles.

Luke waited until I was seated next to Olive before he took a seat in an armchair next to his brother - the two of them immediately struck up a conversation.

Olive smiled. "I'm sorry we missed breakfast with you. Matthew brought some food to the room and ate with me." She smiled gently at her husband. "He's worried about me."

"He loves you," I added with a smile of my own.

"I have a feeling we'll see a lot more of you when we get back to New York. I'm looking forward to that, and for you to meet William. Let me show you a photograph of him." She reached into her large purse and pulled out a small photograph of a chubby two-year-old.

Olive sighed. "I can't wait to get home."

Sipping my tea, I remembered meeting William in 1987. He'd been in his seventies, in good health except for his memory loss. The only time I had really spoken to him was at Luke's funeral.

The tears came fast and sudden and I couldn't blink them away fast enough.

The startled look on Olive's face told me I wouldn't be able to hide my distress from Luke, who quickly snapped his head in my direction.

"Esmé?" Luke put an arm around my shoulders as Olive handed me a white handkerchief.

"I'm sorry," I sniffed, trying to pull myself together. "Seeing that picture reminded me of my friend's little boy. He died just before I left." I hoped they would leave it at that, since I couldn't tell them the truth about my fate. I dabbed at my eyes and patted Luke's cheek. "I'm okay. I really am." I smiled to reassure him. "And, Olive, you have a beautiful son. I'm sorry I broke down on you like that."

"Oh, nonsense." She patted my knee. "These things happen."

Luke still watched me closely but said nothing more before becoming engrossed in conversation with this brother once more.

"Your friend Violet seems to be having fun with Mr. Calder," Olive mentioned. "We saw them playing croquet not long ago."

I chuckled. "Violet is an amazing young woman - full of dreams. I really hope they come true for her someday."

"I have a feeling Mr. Calder will take her away with him when we get to New York." Olive fanned herself. "I'm sure I'll have stories to tell Matthew's mother. First you, turning Luke's head, and then young Violet with Mr. Calder. You're going to love Luke and Matthew's mother. At first, she seems stern, but she is not. She is full of dry wit."

My excitement grew as I listened to Olive talk about New York. I knew *my* New York, of course, but not the New York of 1912. I turned my head to see Luke in profile, and my heart leapt with joy at his closeness. I would do anything to spend the rest of my life with him. I never wanted to leave his side. I wanted seventy-five years with Luke, not four and a half days.

19:00

"What were you thinking before?" Luke asked.

I frowned, wondering to what he referred.

He saw my confusion and offered, "With Olive over tea? You were talking and then you turned and stared at me." He smiled. "I loved the way you looked at me, it was such a soft look and I wondered what you were thinking."

Olive had noticed the way I'd looked at Luke and had raised an eyebrow when I had started the conversation again. We had both ignored it, but I'd known Luke wouldn't.

I moved closer and felt his reaction in the way his chest rumbled with pleasure. With a teasing smile on my lips, I said, "I admitted to myself that I want to spend the next seventy-five years with you."

He stumbled for a moment and cleared his throat. "Is that true?"

"Hmm." I smiled as Luke led us into the dining room. "I hope you don't mind."

"No," he squeaked, clearing his throat again. "I don't mind." His face gradually broke into a delighted grin. "I don't mind at all."

The dining room seemed to be where everyone met to eat and gossip. So many rumors had been spread. Many of them I heard from Violet, who somehow managed to know everything.

"You seem cheerful tonight," Matthew commented to his brother.

"I've got a beautiful woman on my arm, why wouldn't I be cheerful?" Luke winked at me. "Besides, you look just as happy." He grinned. "Something you want to tell me, brother?"

Matthew blushed bright red while his wife and myself chuckled behind our hands.

"What's so amusing?" Violet asked, joining us on James Calder's arm.

"I believe my brother has an announcement to make." Luke grinned, embarrassing Matthew.

I tugged at Luke's hand as he finally sat down next to me. "Leave him alone." I shook my head, a twitch of mirth on my lips.

Matthew sat down and took his wife's hand. "Olive and I are going to be proud parents again."

"I knew it!" Luke slapped his thigh before leaning forward to kiss Olive on the cheek and congratulate his brother. "It's good to be right all the time."

"Don't let him fool you, Esmé," Matthew teased. "He's not always right, I am."

"Oh, stop it," Olive pleaded, laughing. "When they

both get started, it can take a while for them to calm down."

"Hmm, I've seen it happen a few times," James added before turning his attention to Violet.

Luke whispered into my ear, "I'm glad you're here with me, Esmé."

"Me too." I smiled, my hand slipping to his thigh for a few seconds before returning to my own.

"After dinner, we'll look at the stars," he suggested.

"I'd like that."

"So, Esmé," Matthew interrupted, "where are you going when we get to New York?"

Nerves fluttered in my stomach at the question, for I had no idea where my final destination would be. I certainly knew where I wanted it to be. "Well, I think my destination has changed since I boarded the ship," I admitted, my eyes finding Luke's and holding them.

He gave me a dark look before a grin split his face. "If I have my way, Matthew, you'll be seeing a lot more of Esmé."

A robust laugh escaped between Matthew's lips. "I knew that, of course, I just wanted to hear it confirmed. I think Olive would like a friend."

Frowning, I turned to the other woman and searched her face. Questions nagged at me, but I would wait to ask them for now. I did not want to embarrass Olive in front of the others.

"I hope Olive will show Violet and I the best places to shop."

"I'd be delighted. We'll have afternoon tea at the St. Regis," Olive said, leaning over Luke, then whispered, "It's owned by John Jacob Astor. He's a passenger on this ship with his young wife Madeleine. She's pregnant and the gossip is rampant."

"Olive," Matthew warned.

Olive winked and sat up straight in her chair. "Sorry, Luke," she grinned, "I didn't mean to lean over your food." Turning to her husband, she said, "Esmé may not have known."

"Everyone knows." Matthew exchanged glances with his wife as I leaned against Luke's side.

He leaned closer and was surprised when I placed my lips gently against his cheek and whispered in his ear, "Can we really be together in New York?"

"Yes," he answered without hesitation.

"Then we will." After another peck on the cheek, I noticed how quiet Violet had become.

James ate his meal but kept looking at Violet, and that's when I realized what was wrong. The poor girl thought she had to sail back to England.

Reaching out, I put my hand over Violet's to get her attention, and once I had it, I told Violet, "You are in charge of your own destiny, Violet. The plans you had when you boarded this ship can be changed." I looked at Luke with a soft smile on my face and admitted, "Mine have."

I felt the warmth of Luke's hand on my thigh, squeezing it gently at my words. I held Violet's gaze as the young girl pulled herself together.

I turned to James and saw in his eyes how much he liked Violet.

"I think both of your destinies changed when you came aboard this ship," Olive observed.

"Very astute, dear." Matthew motioned for a waiter to refill his wine. "My brother's certainly has." He grinned. "I wish they'd hurry up with the rest of the food so we can celebrate our good news with the finest cigar."

Beside her, Luke groaned. "I hate those smelly things."

"You always have, but you can have a glass of whiskey instead, although I plan on having both."

"Don't you dare get all smelly and drunk, or you'll be sleeping on a lawn chair out on the promenade," Olive told her husband.

"Well, honey, you know those old wooden things give me a bad back."

Luke laughed. "Then you know what to do to prevent that, brother."

A yellow dessert was placed in front of me. It reminded me of the bread-and-butter pudding my grandmother used to make.

Curious, I leaned against Luke. "What is it?"

"Waldorf pudding. Try some, it's really good." He offered me a small amount on his spoon.

A small blush worked its way up my neck and onto my face, but I accepted the offered sweetness, savoring the delicious taste as it slid down my throat. "I've never had it before. It's delicious."

Luke cleared his throat and turned back to his dessert while I ate mine.

It wasn't long before Matthew insisted that both Luke and James join him for a drink.

Luke planted a kiss on my ear and whispered, "I'll find you later."

My smile lit up my entire face, while Luke's eyes sparkled with longing.

"He's so smitten with you," Olive commented. "James with you too, Violet." She clapped her hands together. "You have both met two wonderful men. Of course, I'm not impartial because Luke is my brother-in-law and James is a family friend. It's just that neither of them has ever shown much interest in any of the women my mother-in-law has tried to push at them." Her smile faded and she became solemn. "Please don't hurt them."

"Why would we hurt them?" Violet asked.

"What she means is, when we get to New York, not to disappear without a trace when I think both Luke and James want to keep us with them." I stared after Luke. As if he knew my eyes were on him, he turned his dark head, curiosity in his gaze. "Luke wants me with him and that's where I want to be. I'd be willing to fight my fate for the chance to spend a lifetime with him."

"Oh." Olive sighed. "I'm so glad you feel that way about him. He does too, he can't keep his eyes off you, or his hands for that matter."

"I would have said his lips," Violet muttered.

I met Violet's gaze and laughed. "I would have to agree with the both of you. I feel like I've known him for years." I became serious. "Not just a day. He's in my heart." I pressed the palm of my hand to my chest, tears hovering on my lashes. "And I know he will be until the day I die."

"You made me cry." Olive dabbed at her eyes with a soft handkerchief while Violet looked dazed.

"I think you just described how I feel about James." Violet shook her head and sat back in her chair. "I'm in love with James."

A gasp from behind us made our heads turn, only to find James in shock with a wide, silly grin on his face. Not a word was spoken as he helped Violet out of her seat.

I watched as the two lovers disappeared.

"Bless my heart." Olive pressed a handkerchief to her chest. "How old is she?"

"Eighteen."

"Esmé, please come with me." Luke appeared, as did Matthew to attend to his wife.

"I'll see you both tomorrow." I wrapped my arm around Luke's.

"You will, and thank you for this evening, Esmé. My mind is at peace." Olive glanced at Luke before her smile landed on me. "Good evening."

As soon as we left the dining room, Luke asked, "What was that all about with Olive?"

I gave him a cheeky laugh. "Wouldn't you like to know?" I teased. "It was girl talk."

"Is that so?" His lips twitched. "What if I told you I can read lips, and I really hope I read yours right?"

Shocked, I narrowed my eyes at Luke. "Are you teasing me?"

He laughed. "Let's just say I think it would be wise for me to drop you off at your cabin and say good night."

"Hmm, I don't think I'm ready to say good night just yet." I squeezed Luke's arm. "Will you take me to look at the stars?"

Luke put his arm around my shoulders as soon as we were on deck, then wrapped his dinner jacket around me. "You'll freeze," he commented, holding me close as we walked off to the side.

"I'm glad it's a clear night," I said happily. "I think we should both pick a star and make a wish."

"Pick one." Luke settled behind me, his arm around my waist, as we gazed out across the moonlit night to the soft whoosh of the ship moving through the water.

I wished for a life with Luke.

"I've chosen one and made my wish," I turned and looked up at Luke. "Your turn."

After a long and thoughtful look at me, Luke stared out to sea and closed his eyes. Moments later, they opened.

"I hope our wishes come true," he whispered.

"So do I." I buried my face in his neck, breathing a kiss that made my body tingle from the contact.

Luke murmured against the top of her head, "I really need to take you to your cabin." He kissed my ear and cupped my face in his large hands. "You are precious, Esmé Rogers."

15:00

"MISS?" VIOLET MUTTERED. "ESMÉ."

"That's better." I twirled in the pale pink dress I wore, thanking God I'd managed to avoid the dreaded corset again. "What can I help you with?"

"Do you think I spend too much time with James? I should be working for you."

I shook my head. "I'm really happy for you, Violet. I want you to be happy and if that means spending all your time with James, then that's fine with me." I took Violet's hands in mine. "I don't need help dressing, bathing or cleaning my room." I laughed. "I've been doing all that by myself for years."

"It just doesn't feel right." Violet clarified, "For me to leave you alone."

"Violet," I said annoyed. "All my time is spent with Luke, as it should be." I smiled at the thought of him as warmth filled my body. "I want to talk to him and get to know him better and I wouldn't be able to do that if you were with us." I danced about. "It must be easier for you to be with James without me around, right?"

"I suppose."

I rolled my eyes. "Violet, enjoy being with James. I hope one day we'll both be lucky enough to be married and best friends in New York." I grinned and twirled around the room. "I love this dress."

"It's really very pretty." Violet looked down at her own dress with a mysterious smile. "This is James' favorite color."

I gently cupped the young girl's face. "You are so beautiful, Violet, and please, I beg you, from now on, forget everything before you come aboard this ship. You are Violet Gibson, and what's mine is yours." Almost giddy, I added, "I'm so excited about the future, Violet," before my smile faded.

Violet tilted her head and frowned. "If you're so excited, why do you look so sad?"

Sighing, I sat in the chair and rubbed my cold

arms, suddenly chilled. "Nothing is simple for me. I can't really explain it, and even if I could, I'm not sure anyone would believe me."

"Then talk to Luke. He'll help you." Violet smiled. "He loves you."

"Just like James loves you." I returned Violet's smile and jumped to my feet with a sudden thought. "I know what I'm going to do." I quickly kissed Violet on both cheeks, grabbed a shawl and left the cabin.

In a hurry, I ran to the purser's office, only to be stopped. "John!" My hand clutched at my chest in surprise. "You startled me."

"I need to talk to you, miss." He glanced around, his words urgent.

"Can we talk later?" I asked. "I need to speak to the purser."

John shook his head. "I need to talk to you before you talk to anyone."

I tilted my head to the side and frowned, staring at the boy, wondering why he was so adamant. "I don't understand."

"I know." He sighed. "But if you don't talk to me first, you'll regret not listening."

I opened and closed my mouth. "Um, all right."

He nodded, relieved. "Let's get out of the way. We can't be overheard."

More curious than ever, I hoped Luke wouldn't overhear us talking and get the wrong idea.

Once we were alone, John turned to me. "You can't tell anyone what you know?"

"About what?"

He tugged at his hair. "If you tell anyone about the impending disaster, you will disappear back to where you came from. Everyone here will have no memory of you, but as punishment for trying to interfere with the future, you'll remember, and the disaster you tried to stop will still happen."

"Oh!" I sat down heavily on the bench behind me.

I stared at him, my head spinning as he went on, "I was born in 1734," he answered my unasked question. "I seem to be permanently stuck at seventeen. I only know the future of the Titanic because I've been here before, which makes no sense, but it's the truth. The second time I was on board, I tried to warn the captain, just like you are trying to do. That's why I know what will happen to you if you tell anyone."

"This is all too much."

"Yes, it is. I can't explain it, and I don't even know what I did to go through time, but it keeps happening to me. I'm stuck. I don't want that to happen to you."

"So, I can't tell the captain?"

He shook his head.

"Or Luke." I covered my mouth with a small hand to keep the anguish in my throat.

"No one." He shook his head again. "This will happen no matter what you do or say. The only difference is that if you stay quiet, and assuming you and Luke get back to New York, you can have a life with him. You would have nothing if you tried to tell anyone what you know."

I sat in stunned silence and then asked, "What about after? If I admit to Luke that I knew about it and where I came from after the Titanic sank, will I stay or will I be sent back?"

"As long as you don't interfere with history, you'll be fine. You just can't tell anyone what you know about the future before it happens." He sighed. "No one can interfere with history." He hesitated as if to say more. Then he added, "But the course is not set for anyone." He smiled, wryly. "You set your own future, Esmé, it hasn't been set in stone yet."

My heart pounded as I tried to understand what was being said, but all I felt was confusion. "Are we the only ones?"

John stared at me for a moment. "No, I don't think we are. You're just the only one I've met."

"How did you know?"

"I only suspected it at first, but I've been watching

you. Sometimes you seem lost, out of your element. I went to knock on your cabin just now, and I heard you talking to Violet about not knowing how to explain something. I took a chance."

"And you were right."

"I'm glad I was," John said. He tipped his hat and quickly disappeared.

"So am I," I whispered.

I sat for a long time while my heart thudded. It turned out that I had no control over what would happen in just a few days. All these people would lose their lives in two days, and I couldn't do anything about it. It made me angry that I couldn't change anything.

"I've been looking all over for you," Violet said. "We were all worried, but a crew member told me where to find you. It was strange, but never mind, I have you now."

"Luke?" I whispered, letting Violet lead me back to my cabin.

"He's worried. He's down on the deck looking for you. Let's get you warmed up and then I'll try to find him."

I nodded, slowly beginning to thaw from the shock of my discovery. "I'll be fine, Violet." I turned and pleaded with the other woman. "Please, don't fuss. I really am fine." I smiled reassuringly. "Go spend time with James."

Violet nodded slowly. "If you say so."

"I do, and I really will be fine when I get to the cabin." I leaned forward and kissed Violet's cheek. "Thank you for looking out for me."

Violet smiled and ran back to James.

I clutched my stomach and slumped behind the door as soon as I reached the safety of my cabin.

After my conversation with John, I felt nervous and didn't know what to do. I couldn't talk to Luke either, which I had hoped to do. I hated not being honest about where I came from and what I knew.

19:45

"You gave us quite a scare this afternoon," Matthew commented. "Thought you fell overboard."

"Thanks for reminding me," Luke muttered in a sullen mood.

I glanced at him, but he avoided my gaze. There had been too much commotion when word got out that I was back in my cabin. As soon as everyone had left, I'd knocked on the connecting door, but if Luke had been in there, he'd ignored me.

At the table, I felt the anger coming from him.

When I'd finally had enough, I stood, surprising every-one, including Luke. When his eyes finally met mine, I asked, "Please come with me. I have something to say."

Without another word to the others, Luke took my arm and led me out onto the promenade.

"I'm sorry, Esmé. You had me worried. More than worried, if I'm being honest. Yet you gave no real explanation. I thought your feelings for me were grow-ing, as mine for you."

I swallowed hard. "My feelings for you are deep, Luke. It's not that I don't want to tell you what is going on with me, because I do. Desperately. I just can't. But I promise you, when we get to New York, I will explain everything. I just can't tell you until then, and then I'll explain why." I grabbed the front of his tuxedo. "Until then, you have to trust me. Please."

He watched me carefully; the slight smile on his lips told me he would trust me. "You promise to tell me everything?"

"When we get to New York, I will tell you every-thing. I'll answer all your questions. I will still sound crazy and have no real way to prove anything to you, but I will tell you everything I know."

"Then, as curious as I am, I will trust you to talk to

me when we get to New York." He leaned over and kissed my forehead.

He offered his arm and led me further along the promenade. "Are you hungry?"

"Not really. I was too worried about you not talking to me to have an appetite."

"I was too worried about you to have one." He chuckled. "We make a good couple, don't we?"

"I love us together." I snuggled my face into his arm as we strolled across the deck when I asked, "Would you like to come back to my cabin for a nightcap?"

Luke pulled me aside and forced my eyes to meet his. "Are you sure it is wise for us to be alone together?" He quickly pressed a finger to my lips as I opened my mouth to speak. "I know what I want, and that is to have you in my life for the rest of my days. But I don't want there to be any gossip about you because of me."

I wrapped my fingers around Luke's wrist, pulling his hand away but keeping it in mine. "I want the same thing you do, but I want to be able to relax with you without others watching. I just want to have you all to myself for a while."

He pressed his forehead against mine. "Then we'll

open the adjoining doors, so no one knows. I need to protect you."

"And you," I added.

"I don't care about my reputation, only yours."

"Hmm," I sighed.

"Let's go there now." Luke cleared his throat and took my hand, placing it on his arm. "We're being watched," he murmured.

Within minutes, I was in my cabin. I took a deep breath to calm my nerves, then turned the key in the connecting door to let Luke in. I knew people would think it was wrong, but nothing had ever felt more right. My heart was dancing with excitement. When I opened the door and saw the heartbreaking tenderness of his gaze, a tingle in the pit of my stomach took flight with butterflies.

"To receive such a look of loving tenderness from you fills me with joy." Luke offered a wry smile. "I'm glad we're alone to receive it." He took my hand and pulled me into his cabin. "I have whiskey if you'd like some."

"No, I'm fine." I laughed. "Although I am nervous, so maybe it will calm me down."

"Oh, Esmé. I promise you have nothing to fear from me." He poured us both a finger of the fine Irish liquid and motioned with a nod of his head for me to join him at the small table.

"I'm not afraid of you per se, I'm afraid of what you make me feel, and because of that I'm afraid of what I might do." I looked away before Luke gently took my chin in his hands and turned me back to him.

"That took a lot of courage to say."

I acknowledged his words.

"Well, let me tell you that I feel the same way about you. We only met two days ago, and I think there is something else at work." He laughed. "I've never felt so compelled to be with a woman before - never Esmé. But with you, it's like I'm afraid to take my eyes off you. I have this desperation to tie you to me, so you'll always be with me. It's almost like I'm afraid you'll disappear. The truth is, I've fallen in love with you."

"You have?" I gasped. "I love you too." Without another care or thought, I threw myself out of the chair and into Luke's lap and waiting arms.

I had dreamed of being crushed in his embrace and now I was. It made my heart jump and my pulse pound. The longer he held me, the more I ached for the fulfillment of his lovemaking.

I felt the movement of his heavy breathing against

me and then heard his whispered words, "Marry me, Esmé." His breath was warm and moist against my face, and my heart raced as our passionate gazes met and held. "You are mine, and I want you to be my wife, the mother of my children, and my partner for life. Please tell me now if you don't want that." He stood, pulling me with him, his hands locked against my spine.

Everything I wished for in 1987 was coming true. Even though it scared me, I was going to believe the words I had spoken to Violet about being in charge of one's own destiny.

A large hand moved up to cradle my cheek, concern etched on his handsome face. I offered him an affectionate smile. "I love you, Luke Carlisle, and I want to be all those things to you, your wife, the mother of your children, and your partner for life. I love you." Standing on my tiptoes, I tenderly touched my lips to his.

Luke's kiss was slow and deliberate until our tongues touched, then he took over the kiss, his mouth hungrily covering mine. Suddenly, I was lifted into the cradle of his arms. His kiss sent the pit of my stomach into a wild vortex of desire, and the tight body against mine trembled as our passion grew.

Just as suddenly, his mouth pulled away. Panting heavily, he helped me to her feet before taking a step away and turning his back. I saw the harshness of every breath he took, which seemed to be a struggle. It was hard for me too. I struggled to catch a breath from the desire that coursed through my blood.

The need to touch him, to soothe him, became overwhelming, so I moved up behind him, my arms wrapped around his waist. I rested my face on his back and sighed. "I love everything about you. And I love the way you make me feel," I admitted, breathing out a long sigh of contentment.

Luke squeezed my hands that rested on his stomach before he slowly pulled them away and turned to face me. He took my hands into his and admitted, "My passion for you knows no bounds, but I won't take you to bed until we are married." He kissed my knuckles. "The captain can marry us."

With an amused smile on my face, I teased, "So soon?"

Luke smiled. "We love each other, and when we get off this ship, I want you on my arm as my wife." He grinned.

"You're a romantic man, Luke Carlisle. You fill my heart with so much love, so please arrange our wedding as soon as you can."

He kissed the tip of my nose. "I will speak to the

purser first thing in the morning and see if he can arrange it with the captain."

I pulled him with me to sit on the side of his bed. The occasional jolt of his thigh against mine made my skin tingle. I let my forehead drop to his shoulder with a sigh of pleasure. "I've never been deeply loved before." I tilted my face so I could hold his gaze. "I feel so much love when you look at me when you touch me. I never want that to fade."

"I promise you it will never fade," he exclaimed with intense pleasure, kissing my waiting lips softly.

A huge feeling of relief washed over me as I admitted, "I can't wait to become Esmé Carlisle. I jumped to my feet with a quick kiss. "I want everything with you, Luke. I don't want to be just a housewife. I want to be with you in every way."

"That's what I want, Esmé." Luke followed me to my feet and took off his jacket. He placed it on the back of a chair and fumbled with his bowtie before finally undoing it and taking it off. He tugged at the collar of his softly pleated shirt and opened a few buttons. "I finally feel like I'm not choking. I hate these stiff collars."

My eyes went to the skin he'd exposed between the open collars, and my body ached to touch him there.

He moaned. "I hate to end this evening, but if you

stay much longer, I won't be responsible for my actions." Even as he spoke, his eyes roamed boldly over me.

"I will leave. I hope you'll join me for breakfast?"

"Always, my love." He reached out and lightly caressed my cheek before pulling his hand away. "Always," he murmured.

Before I threw myself into his arms once more, I quickly walked through our connecting doorway, locking my door behind me. The temptation was there to leave them unlocked, but I couldn't do that to him.

Chapter Eleven

April 13th, 1912

07:45

I stepped out of my cabin and looked around quickly when I heard someone hiss further down the corridor. I turned to find John motioning for me to join him.

Checking to make sure Violet wasn't approaching, I quickly made my way to him, out of sight of the other passengers.

"I wanted to make sure you were okay," he whispered, looking odd.

"I'm fine, but you're not. What's wrong?" I frowned, watching him closely.

John sighed and paced in front of me before stopping. "I shouldn't be telling you this, but," he paused, "there's a fire."

My eyes widened in shock. "Where?"

"In the second and third sections, where they keep the coal. The men say it's been raging for three weeks. They finally got a handle on it today and are confident it'll be out soon."

"We shouldn't have sailed," I muttered.

"No, we shouldn't have. Everyone involved was sworn to secrecy. I only found out because I overheard the firemen talking."

"Has this happened when you've been here before?"

"This is the first time I know anything about it, but I suppose so." John looked sick. "The heat from the fire weakened the hull, which I think is why the iceberg tears into it so easily. It might have happened without the fire, but the hull is now severely weakened."

I stared at the young man, wondering if we could use this to our advantage and sabotage the ship. If we did something to stop or slow the ship, we would surely miss the original timeline. History would be changed, and neither John nor I would have told anyone what we knew.

"John," a sharp voice called. "With me!"

The crewman looked sharply at John before giving me a cold stare.

"You better go," I whispered.

"I'll find you again," he muttered and ran off.

I watched as he joined his crewmate. I grimaced when I realized he was being reprimanded for talking to me, a first-class passenger.

08:15

"Why are Luke and James so anxious to talk to the purser this fine morning?" Matthew asked, unable to hide the amusement dancing in his eyes.

Olive took his hand and squeezed it. "Now behave yourself and stop embarrassing Esmé and Violet."

"I'm saving it for Luke." He grinned.

Violet turned a rosy shade of pink at being teased, while I tried not to show my excitement.

The moment we had arrived at breakfast, both Luke and James had apologized before quickly disappearing. I couldn't wait for Luke to return with the details of our wedding. It was happening so fast, but I knew my destiny was with Luke. I had known it since our first meeting in New York back in 1987.

Olive cleared her throat, pulling me out of my

thoughts, and said, "I'm so glad Luke suggested we have dinner here tonight."

We were in the Café Parisien, with its French ivy-covered trellises holding an assortment of climbing plants that reminded me of the courtyard in my childhood home.

A tiered buffet stand sat in the center of the room and contained an abundance of food. The China service sat on sideboards at each end of the room.

"This room feels more relaxed than the saloon." Olive gave a small smile, trying to hide her grimace.

"Are you all right?" I asked, concerned for the other woman who looked as white as chalk.

"A little queasy, but nothing to worry about," she reassured, taking a bite from her small slice of buttered bread. "I just need something in my stomach, that's all."

"The motion of the ship doesn't help. She'll be much better when we get ashore," Matthew added.

I looked at Violet out of the corner of my eye and saw her own excitement reflected back at me. Maybe I could use a chat with Violet sometime during the day. Because if there was one thing I knew about people in the early nineteen hundreds, it was that they weren't as open about intimate relationships as they had been in the eighties.

Gathering my thoughts, I focused on my breakfast, a boiled egg and bread, hiding a yawn behind a hand. I'd had a terrible night's sleep after being with Luke and everything we'd talked about.

But my thoughts weren't just about how I felt about him, I couldn't stop thinking about what would happen on the 14th. I desperately wanted to talk to Luke about what I knew, but I didn't want to risk my future with him. If John was to be believed - and there was no reason not to - then risking everything wouldn't change the outcome of the Titanic.

I looked worriedly at Violet. While my relationship with Luke was written in the stars, I had to make sure Violet was taken care of and that James Calder was a good man.

Luke approached with a grin on his face. It matched the one I caught briefly on James' face.

Luke pulled out the chair next to me and, taking my hand, announced to the table. "The captain is going to marry us tomorrow."

James announced. "And us."

"I just knew what was going on!" Olive grinned. "I just knew."

"Congratulations," Matthew exclaimed in his boisterous voice. "I think the men should sneak off to the smoking room after breakfast to celebrate."

Luke chuckled. "You know I hate that room. I can't breathe."

"I promised Violet another game of croquet after breakfast, and I don't like that room either."

"Boring," Matthew complained. "I'll think of something else." He was not to be outdone. "Eventually!"

Laughing, Luke said, "I'll leave it up to you, brother, but right now I'm pretty hungry."

He went to get some breakfast while I finished mine, wondering if we would live to be married more than a day.

"Violet, I think we need to get together this afternoon with Olive to decide what we are going to wear for our weddings." I squeezed Violet's hand. "I'm sure the men can find something to keep them entertained for a few hours."

"Oh, that will be fun!" Olive exclaimed. "I actually have just the dresses for you two." She grinned, more color in her face. "A friend of mine asked me to bring her five different wedding dresses from London. They're originally from Paris. I'll tell her I misplaced two."

"A convenient friend," Matthew grumbled.

"Oh, hush!" Olive blushed.

"No need. I will gladly reimburse you for Esmé's

dress," Luke said between bites of breakfast, glancing at his sister-in-law.

"Of course, I will do the same for Violet's dress." James covered Violet's hand on the table. "I want to do that for my bride." He grinned. "You agreed to marry me, so I have to thank you in some way."

"Oh! You don't have to thank me. I love you," Violet confessed, more confident than I had ever heard her.

"When I married Olive, I thanked her in a different—*ouch!*" Matthew turned and glared at his wife while Olive ignored him, a blush spreading across her cheeks.

I chuckled from behind my handkerchief and briefly caught Luke's amused gaze. I had to turn away before I lost myself in a fit of giggles.

"Isn't it obvious that William was born nine months after our wedding?" Matthew added, pleased with himself for getting the last word.

Luke rolled his eyes. "I think I should pity your wife for being married to you. Can't you keep a secret?"

Olive groaned. "I think we should change the subject." She smiled. "I also think a few nights on the floor for my husband might keep his mouth shut." She turned to Matthew. "Wouldn't you say so, dear?" She patted his hand.

"I think the threat is enough," Matthew grumbled. "I'd break my back sleeping on the floor."

Luke threw back his head and laughed. "Showing your age, brother." He laughed.

"I'm only three years older than you." Matthew pointed his finger.

Luke chuckled and finished his breakfast in relative silence.

"If you'll excuse us," James got up and helped Violet to her feet. "I'll bring her back after lunch so you ladies can have some fun without any interference from us men."

"I look forward to that," I said, quickly squeezing Violet's hand.

Violet beamed as she was led away. She looked absolutely smitten with James, which made my heart so much lighter. Knowing that the young girl I had quickly taken a liking to would be taken care of made it easier for me to focus on Luke. I was determined to have the life I craved with my husband by my side.

I'd always thought there was something missing in my relationship with Jake, and now, after meeting Luke, I had been right. I had never been completely relaxed with Jake. Always waiting for something to happen, never feeling at ease with him. From the moment I met Luke, even in New York, I recognized him. Since we had been on the ship, it was as if my whole being had recognized him as my own.

14:30

"I trust the croquet went well, James?" I drawled as Violet entered my room, looking as if she were in a dream.

"Oh yes, miss," Violet took a chair at the table, a silly smile playing on her lips. "I'm glad you changed your mind about me being allowed to show what I'm feeling." She sighed.

I laughed, amused. "I'm happy for you, Violet. Just please stop calling me Miss. It's Esmé."

Violet sat up straight, a sudden change in her demeanor before she burst into tears. One minute she was happy, the next she looked like her heart was broken. "Violet?" I asked, crouching at Violet's feet. "What is it?"

"James doesn't know I'm your maid. I have to tell him before the wedding so he can change his mind."

"Oh," I smiled, encouraging, "I've seen the way he looks at you. He won't change his mind once he knows the truth. Besides, the truth is that you are my friend.

You have never lied to him, so please remember that. I know you didn't tell him how you ended up on this ship, but you didn't lie either."

She nodded in agreement. "I just told him the truth."

"Then I don't think you have anything to worry about." I patted her knee before standing up. "Olive will be here soon. Why don't you dry your face and stop thinking so hard."

Violet tilted her head. "Did you tell Luke what was on your mind?"

That took me by surprise and I shook my head gently with pain in my heart. "I don't know how, but I promised Luke, I would tell him everything as soon as we got to New York. There's a reason I can't tell him now, but he told me he trusts me. Once we're on land and settled, I'm going to tell him everything about me. No matter how big or small, I trust in our love that he will accept everything."

"I need to be more trusting," Violet admitted. "I know James loves me, and I have to believe that. I hope that if I tell him, his love for me will make everything okay."

"That's the spirit, Violet." I danced to the door when I heard a knock.

Olive walked in with two maids behind her. They

were laden down under piles of silk. "Put them on the bed," Olive urged. "Thank you."

I turned away so as not to embarrass anyone while Olive sent them on their way with a tip.

The pile of silk on the bed overflowed, and I noticed that Violet was mesmerized by the white silk and lace dress. My eyes kept going back to the other dress, which had a lot of fabric. The color reminded me of vanilla ice cream.

"I see you both picked out your dresses without me," Olive gushed. "Violet, you have to try on the white one right now!"

"Oh, but I don't know." Violet bit her lip, unsure.

"You will look so beautiful in the white dress, Violet. Please try it on before you make a decision." I chuckled. "Although I think if Olive has her way, you'll be wearing the dress."

"Esmé and I will get the dress ready for you. Go and take that dress off." Olive turned to Violet. "Hurry, I'm so excited."

Violet turned and hesitated only a moment before walking into the dressing room.

"She's so young," Olive commented, picking up the white lace dress. "But she's so in love, and so is James, and that's all that matters." She smiled. "I was hoping you would choose the other dress. It was made for you."

"It looks beautiful." I looked at the beautiful vanilla fabric again.

With twinkling eyes, Olive said, "It's bolder than anything I've seen before, so I couldn't resist it." She leaned closer and whispered, "I bought a new dress in pale pink, which is also more daring. Apparently, it's a new fashion that's about to hit America. Matthew hasn't seen me in it yet." She blushed. "If I wasn't already pregnant, I would be after wearing that dress."

I blinked and began to laugh. "I'm curious now."

"Hmm, what do you think of Violet's choice?" Olive held up the lovely dress.

"It's plain and simple, so very pretty. This is perfect for Violet." Bending, I took hold of the hem, and the dress was soft to the touch, with layers of the finest silk. "I can't wait to see her in it."

"I'm afraid to touch such beauty," Violet admitted as she came out of the dressing room in her undergarments. She looked self-conscious, so I quickly pulled her over to where we were standing and helped Olive pull the dress over Violet's head.

"It fits, too." Olive continued to fasten the delicate buttons at the back.

I watched Olive and asked, "Olive, what did

Matthew mean about you having a convenient friend? I don't mean to pry, but it's been on my mind."

Olive sighed and looked sad as she tucked a strand of blonde hair behind her ear. "I have a problem keeping my mouth shut. I'm all for manners, but if I don't agree with something, I say so. I've lost friends because of it, and now I only see them when I'm useful to them."

"The lady you bought the clothes for. She's one of them?"

Olive nodded her head as she turned Violet toward the mirror. "You look like a princess, Violet."

She did look like a princess! The cut of the dress was perfect for the girl, and the color brought out the warmth of her skin. I looked up at the vanilla-colored mountain of silk. "My turn," I said, turning to the dressing room.

I would leave Olive alone for now, but once we were in New York together, I was determined to make sure Olive had only *real* friends. I had been known to speak my mind once or twice, and I wouldn't have a problem doing so when I got to New York, even if it was 1912.

"What's taking you so long?" Violet shouted. "You never take this long to get dressed."

Rolling my eyes, I stepped into the room and

gasped when I saw myself in the mirror. The dress was low on the chest and back, fitted at the waist, with yards of material flowing from the waist down.

"I knew this was for you when I went through the dresses this morning." Olive moved closer. "Why did you take off your corset?" Olive frowned.

Violet giggled and grinned. "I told you, ladies always wear a corset."

Olive looked between us, so I volunteered, "The thought of wearing one causes me pain, so I definitely don't wear one. They scare me."

"You're serious?" Olive asked doubtfully.

"Yes." I ran my hand down my torso while Olive adjusted the ribbons. It was so beautiful, and I was right about it being low in the front and back. I would have to find something else to wear under the dress because my chemise was showing.

"Turn to the side," Olive asked. "Stay like that." She grabbed the material at the back of the dress and pulled it toward the floor. "There's so much material at the back of the dress, it's like a train."

Standing back, Olive admired her handiwork. "Esmé, you look stunning." She grinned. "I can't wait to see Luke's face when he sees you." She turned to Violet. "James will faint when he sees you." She dabbed at her eyes and hugged Violet and I. "I'm getting two sisters tomorrow. It makes me so happy."

I watched the other woman. Fighting my own tears, I wanted to hug Olive tightly. If history repeated itself, Olive would not survive the sinking. She would die with her husband and unborn child.

Tears trickled down my cheeks, and when Olive and Violet gasped, I let them believe they were tears of emotion over the dress. Not because my heart was breaking over the very real possibility that Olive would die in the sinking. What would happen to Violet and James?

16:00

"Do you know that boy?" Luke asked, pointing at John as we walked along the promenade. "I've seen him a few times, watching us, but he never comes close."

I gave John a nervous look before plastering a smile on my face. "It's John. He helped me find my cabin when we set sail from Southampton. I was lost and a little disoriented. He was really very kind."

"Well, I think he has his eye on my lady."

If only it were that simple.

"Oh, stop!" I squeezed Luke's arm. "I'm sure he

has a girl back home, if not on this ship." We moved to the side of the ship, and I leaned over to watch the ship crash through the waves. "I never thought I'd be aboard such a fine ship, or that I'd meet the man of my dreams."

Luke moved behind me, shielding me as his hands landed on my hips. He whispered in my ear, "You have become everything to me very quickly, Esmé. I can't wait to make you, my wife. You'll be the most beautiful bride." He kissed my cheek.

I gave a mysterious smile. "When you see me tomorrow in the dress Olive picked out for me, you won't be able to talk because I'll leave you breathless." I spoke boldly and confidently.

His hand slipped around my waist, and he pulled me close. "You always leave me breathless." His lips traced a blaze of fire along my neck as he nuzzled my hair out of the way. "I love you, Esmé."

I would never get tired of hearing those words, and I prayed with all my heart that they would survive the sinking together. Luke had, and I wanted to change my own story. I never wanted to go back to 1987, no matter what I knew about World War I, the Depression, and all the rest. My life was intertwined with Luke's, and I would do anything to keep it that way.

"Why are you so thoughtful? Did I frighten you?" Luke asked, his voice heavy with worry.

I took his hands in mine and intertwined our fingers. I turned my head and looked over my shoulder. "I'm thinking about how much I want to spend the rest of my life with you. I want to see New York through your eyes. I want to have afternoon tea with Olive and Violet at the St. Regis. I want to have dinner with you at Delmonico's." I turned in his arms and shivered as his hands landed on my bottom before he quickly moved them to my hips. "I want so much to be with you, Luke."

"You know Delmonico's?" he asked. "It's one of my favorite restaurants."

"I didn't know that, but Delmonico's has been in New York since the 1800's." I grinned. "Word travels."

"It does." He shook his head. "You make me think anything is possible."

"Anything is possible," I whispered. "As long as we're together."

"Can I take your photograph?" a voice interrupted.

Luke grinned. "As long as you let me purchase it afterwards."

"You can, sir." The man set up his equipment.

Luke put his arm around me, and the photograph

was taken of my upturned face staring at the man I loved.

The photographer disappeared discreetly.

Luke kissed my forehead and asked, "Do you want to go inside and join the others?"

"I think I'd rather push two chairs together and sit out here with you." Taking his hand, I led him over and did exactly as I suggested. I grabbed two of the thick brown blankets and wrapped one around my shoulders and the other over my legs. Luke pulled one over his legs as well.

"You like the outdoors?" he observed, looking out over to the horizon.

"I do." She turned on her side to face him. "What do you usually do to relax?"

"Read. Whatever I can get my hands on. I read the newspaper at breakfast, and then after dinner I read a few chapters of a book; Thomas Hardy and Yeats, to name a few."

"Ah, poetry too. I read Yeats a while ago." I smiled. "I'm afraid it went in one ear and out the other." I wrinkled my nose and Luke laughed.

"So, what do you like to read?" He chuckled.

"Why the laugh, Mr. Carlisle?" I poked him in the stomach.

He chuckled. "Tell me?"

I rolled my eyes as I went through the list of my favorite authors. I couldn't think of anyone who was published—or even born—before 1912. "Bronte," I suggested, hoping he hadn't actually read *Bronte*. I hadn't read the author myself. In my day, I preferred Robert Crais, Sydney Sheldon, Tom Clancy, and Stephen King.

"Olive likes to read the Brontës. So does my mother." He stroked my cheek. "What else do you like besides books, my beautiful fiancée?"

"Hmm," I moved closer until his arms wrapped around my body and he snuggled me against his side, "I love strong coffee, and dessert I could eat for any meal."

He laughed and teased, "I may have noticed that," before giving me a long kiss on my forehead.

"I love to dance when I'm in your arms," I continued. "In fact, I think you've become my new addiction." I turned serious and tilted my face up to his. "I can't stop thinking about you, Luke. It scares me how quickly you've become my whole world."

"Oh, Esmé," he breathed a kiss on my cheek before tucking my face into the curve of his neck, "you humble me. From the moment we met, our connection was strong and pulsating with life. We barely spoke two words before I kissed you."

I smiled against his neck, remembering. "Our lives will change tomorrow," I began nervously, "and I want you to know that I love you. I love you so much and I will for eternity and beyond."

I felt his reaction to my words, pressing into my stomach. I had probably gone too far, but I had to get those words out. It was important to me that Luke knew how much I loved him. I wasn't sure if I would survive much longer than my wedding day.

"I will be nowhere else but at your side, Esmé." He kissed the top of my head. "I promise."

I hoped he would be able to tell me the same on April 16th.

23:20

A knock on my cabin door woke me from a deep sleep. I felt disoriented, but another knock made me jump out of bed and grab my robe from the chair.

"Who is it?" I whispered.

"John."

Startled, I started to open the door when John quickly slipped through, closing the door behind him. "I can't be seen."

"What's wrong?"

"The fire is out." He went to my balcony and looked out into the dark night. "I don't know what to do. I can't tell anyone, but it's tiring to watch the disaster over and over again. I'm not sure how many more times I can do it."

"There must be a trigger or a reason why you keep appearing at the same point in time."

"No matter what I do to make sure I'm not in the same place that I was the last time the Titanic sank, I always end up back on the ship in Southampton."

I fidgeted with the belt of my robe. "I've been thinking. What if we did something to slow the ship down? Rupture the timeline as we know it? That might even help you."

John stared at me as if he hadn't heard me right.

"Think about it, John. We wouldn't have told anyone." I perched on the end of a chair.

"I don't know enough about how the ship works to stop it from moving," he admitted slowly.

"What about dropping the anchor as we get closer? It would take time to pull it back up."

John shook his head. "Not sure that would work. It takes quite a few men to work the anchor." John grumbled and headed for the door. "We'd still be messing with history." With his hand on the doorknob, he said over his shoulder, "I'll think of something. I can't be on this ship again."

"Hmm." I sighed.

He slipped out as quickly as he'd slipped into the room, leaving me uneasy.

"Do you think time passes at the same speed there?" Jake asked Sienna, but it was more of a spoken thought.

"If it passes at the same speed, then the Titanic has already sunk. It's been two weeks, Jake."

"We're assuming she appeared the day the Titanic left Southampton. What if she went back before the Titanic sailed?" Jake watched Sienna, trying not to be distracted by how beautiful she was.

He'd noticed Sienna in the restaurant that night and had been horrible to Esmé when he was angry at himself. He should not have been thinking about Sienna or any other woman while he was with his fiancée.

Sienna blushed as Jake's gaze fell on her face. She couldn't help it, especially since she found him attractive. She looked down and cleared her throat. "We need to go back to the library and see if her name is on any of the passenger lists." She sighed. "I should have done that before you knocked on my door. I was just scared in case she was on the list of the dead."

"It's hard to wrap my head around it. Of course, I want her to be alive, but if she is, does that mean she's going to stay there and spend seventy-odd years with Luke? Does that mean our whole timeline is screwed up? Or does she somehow come back with no memory and that's why Luke has been waiting all these years to tell her to come back to him?" Jake ran his hands through his hair. "I think I might be going crazy."

"Join the club," William said as he walked into the room.

"William!" Sienna jumped up and hugged him. "How was lunch with David?"

"Boring," he replied dryly. "He tells me the same thing every week." He dropped into an armchair. "I think he's the crazy one." He laughed. "So," he met Jake's gaze, "why are you going crazy?"

"Long story."

"Does it have anything to do with that photograph I found the other day?"

"Very perceptive." Sienna moved to sit beside to Jake. "Are you sure that's the only photograph you've seen with Esmé in?"

"I've thought about it." He tapped his finger on his lip. "I was two when I lost my parents, so I don't remember that time. But I know I've seen photographs taken around that time. I'm just not sure where my father kept them. I've looked." He threw up his hands and sighed. "I'm not sure where else they could be unless they're in the attic. There's a lot of dust up there."

"I forgot about the attic." Sienna looked at Jake. "Luke used to move things up to the attic all the time, and I heard a lot of his personal stuff was up there." Sienna swung her leg, her shoe dangling from her slender foot.

Jake forced his gaze away and focused on William, who gave him a knowing grin before clearing his throat. "I think you two should go up there and look around. I'm too old for those narrow stairs."

"I know where the door is, but I've never been up there."

"There's a lot of history up those stairs."

Sienna looked at Jake, then back at William. "What's the first thing you remember?"

"I knew this was coming." He chuckled. "I have a

vague memory of being a kid and playing with wooden blocks. Of my father playing ball out back." He tilted his head toward the backyard. "I remember asking my grandmother why my father always looked sad. I always thought I'd done something wrong. Or that he was mad at me for having to adopt me. She told me he wasn't mad at me, but I didn't believe her."

He shrugged, his gaze becoming thoughtful. "What I told you before, about finding a small box and my father explaining about the woman he loved, I felt sad for him, but I also remember feeling relieved. I finally knew that he wasn't angry with me, he was just sad." He frowned. "What does my father's Esmé have to do with the one I met at his funeral?"

"It's really complicated, and you'll think we're both crazy if I tell you."

"Like I said, I'm already crazy."

"William, if you can remember what you have, then you're not crazy."

William offered a wry smile. "Thank you for that."

"So," Sienna smiled, "I think I'll make you a cup of that lemon tea you like, and then Jake and I will go up to the attic."

"You do that. Bring some flashlights, I'm not sure the lights still work."

"We will." Sienna got up and pulled Jake with her. "Kitchen." She nodded her head. "Tea coming up."

They ran to the kitchen and Jake watched Sienna in silence as she made the tea. The scent of lemon reached his senses and made his nose twitch.

"What do you think we're going to find up there?" he asked.

"Maybe more photographs of Esmé – some kind of proof that she made it off the ship. I really don't know, but I'm impatient to get up there."

"I'm nervous. I want to believe that she made it off the ship. But what if she didn't? Or what—" He dropped his face into his hands. "I don't know what anymore. I just want to know how it all ends. It plays over and over in my head. I want to be able to move on," Jake made sure his eyes held Sienna's, so she knew exactly what he meant before he continued, "and I need all of this to be over."

Sienna stopped what she was doing and walked over to Jake. She wrapped her arms around his waist and tilted her face to his. "I understand what you're saying, Jake. I'm not going anywhere."

A cleared throat from the doorway quickly pulled them apart and they turned to face William.

"I just remembered something," the older man said thoughtfully.

"My father didn't have many friends, but there was one who used to visit him from time to time when I was little. After her visit, he'd be solemn for a few days before he'd snap out of it." He sat down at the table in the kitchen and Sienna and Jake joined him.

"She was a little younger than him. When I was younger, she used to visit with her husband. He died about twenty years ago. She continued to visit after he died, but I never really got to know her well. She's in a residential facility now. I think the lawyer called her when my dad died." He tapped his finger on his lips. "Violet Calder!" He snapped his fingers. "My memory isn't as bad as I thought."

"You're full of surprises, William." Sienna grabbed his hand that was resting on the table. "Do you remember how she knew Luke?"

"I remember that. She boarded the Titanic in Southampton as a maid and arrived in New York on the Carpathia with her husband, James Calder, who was a family friend."

Jake stared at William and asked, "Do you know how old she is?"

"Not really, but at best I'd say she was in her nineties." He shrugged. "I can get you the address from the lawyer if you want to pay her a visit."

"That would be great, William," Sienna muttered,

already forming questions in her head, the attic forgotten.

Chapter Thirteen

April 14th, 1912

07:20

I AWOKE AFTER TOSSING AND TURNING ALL NIGHT. My heart was pounding with a tremendous sense of loss, and if John was to be believed, there was nothing I could do about the impending disaster. I had to believe him because he knew more than I.

How could I get through today knowing what would happen to the ship in the early hours of the next morning? Or would John find a way to prevent it?

"Rise and shine." Violet burst into my room. "It's our wedding day."

In that moment, I knew I would get through the day because I had to. I was marrying the man I loved, and no matter what happened next, he was going to be my husband.

I had to concentrate on the present. I would worry about the future later. "Why aren't you jumping for joy and bursting with excitement?"

"I will be later. I had a bad night's sleep."

"Too excited, I guess," Violet muttered. "I was going to tell James about being a maid today, but I blurted it out last night." She grinned and sat down on the bed beside me. "Turns out he suspected it. He said he didn't care how I came to be on the ship, as long as I disembarked as his wife."

"I'm happy for you." I squeezed the girl's arm. "And now that I'm more awake, I feel refreshed and ready for anything." I stretched and threw off the blankets. "I'm skipping church this morning because I want to move all my things into Luke's room. We'll get fresh linens in here. James and you can have this room."

"Oh! You can't do that," Violet said, horrified.

"Violet, I happen to know that James has a single room, which means you two will be more comfortable in here with this nice big bed," I smiled and turned away while Violet got her blush under control.

"But—"

"No buts, Violet." I turned back and gently took

Violet's hands in mine, pulling her toward the bed. "I don't want to embarrass you, but do you know what to expect on your wedding night?"

Violet turned the color of the strawberries we had eaten the day before and shook her head gently.

"Don't be afraid or embarrassed. Just enjoy his touch. He'll want to please you as much as you'll want to please him."

"It's supposed to hurt," Violet whispered.

"Not always. Sometimes there's a little discomfort, but after the first time it won't hurt. It's a way for two people to share their love for each other. It's supposed to be beautiful." I smiled softly and kissed Violet on the cheek. "Now." I jumped to my feet. "No more talk of refusing this room. Consider it a wedding gift if you wish. However, I plan to share Luke's room from now on."

I quickly disappeared into the dressing room, closing the door behind me before Violet could see the anguish, which was sure to be on her face.

My legs gave way as I sat on the floor and looked around the small room. It would be another seventy-three years before the ship would be seen again.

Why hadn't I learned more about the Titanic after meeting Luke? I should have. Maybe I would have discovered a lifeboat that took men as well as women and children. Maybe I would have found out if I had survived. So many thoughts, and although I couldn't say anything, I could prepare everyone later that evening. Make sure the six of us got off the ship before it was too late.

Holding on to the dresser, I pulled myself up and looked into the mirror. I was pale. Too pale for someone whose wedding day it was.

If I didn't pull myself together, Luke would know something was wrong, he might even think I had changed my mind about marrying him. That couldn't happen.

My stomach in knots, I quickly dressed and slipped my feet into a pair of boots. The items on the dressing table were collected and placed in a box.

"Violet, can you help me with the clothes, please?" I grabbed a handful of dresses and moved to drop them on the bed. "We need to sort them. Split them up. You need your own things." I spun around. "We'll do that now. Everything I'm giving you can stay in the closet, and the things I'm taking to Luke's room can go on the bed for now. We still have a few hours before the wedding."

"I could use something to eat," Violet confessed, pressing her hand to her stomach.

"I forgot about breakfast. Let's grab something

quickly, and then we can come back and finish sorting before we have to get dressed."

"That's a good idea." Violet grinned and was first out the door. "Um, don't you think you should brush your hair first?"

I reached up and realized that I'd forgotten every-thing in my rush to get into Luke's room. "Oh! One moment."

I ran back into the dressing room, quickly brushed my hair, and applied some moisturizer. At least I had some color now because the moisturizer was tinted a light pink.

"I'm ready." I turned and curtsied to Violet. "Let's go eat."

I slipped my arm through Violet's and led the girl to the dining room. My mind wouldn't stop racing, it wouldn't let me forget the events ahead of the *ship of dreams*.

"Good morning, Miss."

My eyes darted to the left and found John standing in the hallway.

"Morning, John. This is my friend, Violet."

He tilted his head toward her, but his eyes were on me. "You can help, but not interfere." He held my gaze and I nodded to let him know I understood.

I tugged Violet into breakfast.

"What did he mean?" Violet asked, her eyebrows knitted together.

I glanced behind me, but he was gone. Turning back to Violet, I told her, "I asked him something yesterday, but he was called away before he could answer." I smiled and patted Violet's hand. "I assure you, everything is fine."

"Hmm," Violet muttered, choosing eggs and toast for breakfast.

With a heavy sigh, I followed, hoping my appetite would return. It was difficult - knowing that more than half of the people in the room with us wouldn't be alive come morning.

15:00

My heart pounded as I waited outside the room with Matthew. The cold chill brought goosebumps to my flesh. He had been chosen to give me away as there was no one else. "You both look beautiful," Matthew said as we approached. Violet's cheeks flushed at the compliment. "No need to be nervous. My brother loves you," he said to me, then turned to Violet. "And James loves you." He chuckled. "They should rename the Titanic the Love Boat." He straightened his tuxedo.

I looked at Matthew, startled, and had flashbacks to the television show of the same name, which I had spent many evenings watching. At least now, I had settled nerves. The brief return to the 1980s was beneficial.

"I'm excited about marrying Luke. I'm just a little bit nervous."

"They're ready for you," the ship's purser announced.

I put my hand on my stomach and took a deep breath. A calm I hadn't felt all morning settled over me as Matthew offered his arm to Violet and the three of us walked through the doors.

The number of passengers in attendance surprised me, but the moment my eyes landed on Luke, he was all I saw. He took my breath away, standing tall and handsome in a tuxedo that fit his large frame perfectly. His hair was slicked back and the look on his face was one I would never forget.

We may have only met a few days ago, but our feelings were very real, and I knew that what we had would last beyond anything else.

The captain cleared his throat to get the attention of everyone in the room. His words ran together as I lost my concentration when I saw the tender love in Luke's eyes. I wasn't sure how long the vows lasted, I just knew that the moment the captain pronounced us man and wife, my love for Luke was beyond anything I had ever known.

The passengers cheered as Luke pulled me into his arms for a rather tame kiss. As he pulled away and brushed his lips gently against mine, he whispered, "Hello, Mrs. Carlisle.

I smiled. "Hello, my husband."

Luke's hand trembled as he gently caressed my cheek before we turned to James and Violet. They'd gotten married right beside us, and I felt guilty for not paying more attention to them, until now, when I took my friend into my arms.

"Congratulations." We two exchanged hugs, while James and Luke shook hands with each other, the captain, and the purser.

Luke took my hand and my heart felt full to bursting. The temptation to pinch myself made my fingers twitch. Our wedding day was April 14, 1912. I was born in 1962, although I'd signed the marriage license 1886. I just had to keep the date in mind - it was almost too much to keep straight.

Passengers offered good wishes, and as Luke led me through them, I wondered what condition we would all be in later. Assuming I was one of the lucky ones and Luke didn't lose me in the ocean. How many of the smiling faces would I see on the Carpathian?

I tried to keep the smile on my face, but it became difficult and forced. I was happy. Happier than I could ever remember being. I had married my soulmate. The man I had first met in the future, and the man who had completed me in the past. It was difficult to comprehend, and something told me not to even try.

"Are you all right, Esmé? You've gone pale." Luke touched my cheeks with cool fingers.

I reached up and wrapped a small hand around his wrist. "I am well and so happy to be your wife." I smiled, and it reached my eyes, a real smile for my very real husband. "I love you," I whispered, tilting my face up to his for a lingering kiss.

"The captain has invited us to dinner at his table tonight," Violet gushed. "It will be fun."

I hid my amusement from Violet and laughed at the look on James' face. I thought he had other ideas for the rest of the day, just like I had with Luke.

"I'm sure we can make dinner." Luke pulled a pocket watch out of his jacket. "It's about four hours to dinner." He grinned. "I suggest we go our separate ways until then."

"A good idea," James agreed.

After a group photograph, I slipped my hand into

Luke's and with a gentle tug, made him move with me. I snuggled up against his arm. "I'm so happy right now, Luke."

"I'm holding the most beautiful bride in the world; I couldn't be happier." He put an arm around my shoulders. "Your clothes look really good hanging in the closet with mine."

I grinned. "I knew they would. I just hope James and Violet don't feel uncomfortable using my cabin. It's not like I need it now."

"Don't worry. I've already talked to James about it, and he's really okay with changing rooms. He knows that his room, even though it is a stateroom, isn't big enough for the two of them." He planted a sweet kiss on my cheek. "I'm just looking forward to not having to be away from you at night. I missed you when we parted."

"No more." I sighed and followed Luke to his room.

16:00

As soon as we were behind the closed door of our cabin, Luke encircled me, one big hand on my stomach. The pulse in my neck pounded with excitement and my heart raced, wanting, and needing my handsome husband.

"I'm nervous," he admitted, burying his face in my neck. "I shouldn't admit this to you."

"Oh, Luke! If you can't admit it to me, who can you admit it to?" I turned and wrapped my arms around him, delighted when he shivered in response.

"I've never done this before." Luke offered a wry smile.

I blinked up at him. "You haven't?"

He laughed, embarrassed. "I've never been interested in loveless coupling."

I was thrilled by his declaration and pressed my soft curves against the hard contours of his strong body. "I'm glad."

"I want to be gentle with you," he confessed, his hands trembling as his fingers caressed my neck and shoulders.

The mere touch of his hand sent a warm shiver through me as I gasped. "I love having your hands on me, but I want them on more of me." I pulled away from his touch and slowly unfastened the ribbon at the front of my dress. "I don't want to disappoint you," I confessed, holding his gaze.

"You could never fail me, Esmé. My love for you is unconditional. I love you now, and I will love you when you're with my child. My love will never end. As he spoke, he'd removed the top part of his clothes, his arousal obvious as my eyes caressed him.

I let the cream-colored dress drop around my feet. The only sound in the room was Luke's ragged breathing as I stood naked before him.

"So beautiful," he whispered, quickly removing the rest of his clothes. "I've never seen anyone as beautiful as you are right now, and you're all mine."

"Yes, I am." My breasts heaved as he moved slowly toward me.

His fingers roamed intimately over my breasts, the rosy peaks hardening to pebble hardness at the gentle touch. He took my hand, drawing it hesitantly to himself, and I felt the smooth skin over his hardness.

Luke gasped and shivered at my touch, giving me an intoxicating sensation. I raised my other hand and ran my fingers through the hair on his chest. His whole body shivered seconds before I found myself pressed against his chest - his mouth pressed against mine.

The feel of his chest rubbing against my sensitive breasts made me squirm in his arms. I wanted and needed more, and through the urgency of his touch, so did he.

My need grew as Luke took three steps to the large bed and laid me down beneath him. He held me gaze and slowly moved down, fondling a breast, its pink nipple marble hard. He kissed the other firm nipple, bringing a melting sweetness to me. His tongue burned a path down my ribs to my belly and further down, sending currents of desire through me.

He took my hands, encouraging them to explore him. I caressed the length of his back as he moved over me.

"So beautiful, Esmé," he whispered as he pulled me into his warm, pulsing body. I arched instinctively towards him, welcoming him into my body. His hardness electrified me with a pleasure that was pure and explosive.

My body melted against his. My world was filled with him. My Luke. My husband. Together we found the pace that bound our bodies in exquisite harmony.

A moan of ecstasy slipped from my lips and the feel of his rough skin against mine assaulted my senses. Love flowed inside me like warm honey as I was propelled beyond the point of no return, crying out for release.

We soared higher and higher until we reached the peak of pleasure and we both exploded in a downpour of fiery sensations. Waves of ecstasy pulsed through us before contentment and peace.

Luke sighed in pleasant exhaustion as I snuggled against him, our legs intertwined.

"That was—"

"Beautiful," I finished his sentence, my head resting on his chest as my fingers played with his chest hair.

"I want to spend the rest of our time aboard this ship just like this," Luke whispered into my hair. "I don't want real life to intrude until we have to disembark."

I wiggled higher and buried my face in the curve of his neck, knowing I would have to get Luke into warm clothes later that evening. I might not be able to tell him what was going to happen in a few hours, but I could prepare him and our friends and family.

"You've gone quiet," he observed hesitantly.

To take his mind off my distraction, I distracted him instead, breathing a kiss against his neck. "I didn't sleep well last night because I was so excited about today. I'm pleasantly tired and don't want to move from your arms."

"At least we agree on that." He wrapped a lock of hair around his finger and tugged. "I could leave, apologize for not joining the others for dinner, and then bring back some food?"

I smiled. "I'd like," I kissed his jaw, "to have a

wedding dinner with Violet, James, your brother and his wife." I blushed slightly. "Besides, when your mother asks what we did on our wedding day, I'd rather have something to tell her that won't make us blush."

He chuckled. "Yeah, that would be tricky, although I'm sure my mother would never ask that question, but it would be nice to eat with everyone, I guess."

Tickling his side, he wiggled and laughed while I chuckled. "You could sound more excited."

"I am very enthusiastic," he growled, rolling me onto my back before slipping into the warmth of my body, "for you."

Chapter Fourteen

1987

"I can't believe Violet and Luke spent a few years together in the same nursing home."

"Until a few weeks ago, you had no real interest in the Titanic." Jake shrugged. "Maybe you'll recognize her and remember her when we see her."

"Maybe." Sienna hesitated at the last step that would take them inside. "I'm nervous, Jake. What if she tells us that Esmé died in the sinking? I think it would break my heart."

"Not knowing is killing me," he admitted. "Come on, let's go and find out." He opened the door and led them inside to the large reception desk.

"Who are you here to see?" the nurse asked, looking half asleep.

"Violet Calder," Jake said, pulling the sign in the book toward him to add their names, while Sienna looked around curiously.

She could see a comfortable common area with couches and chairs in the room beyond the reception. The same grumpy nurse led them down a long, wheel-chair-accessible corridor. A special events board for the home, listing movie nights and bingo, was on the wall opposite the door they'd entered. There weren't many decorations until they got further into the house.

A massive aquarium sat at one end of the cafeteria, with silk flower arrangements covering the tables. The TV room's noise could be heard in the hallway, but they walked a few feet past it and came to a halt.

"She's in there. Been expecting you." The nurse walked away, leaving them looking at each other.

"What if—"

"Shh." Jake covered her mouth. "There are no what ifs, okay? We're going to go in there and have a real conversation with her."

Sienna held his gaze, knowing he was right. "I can do this."

"We can do this," Jake muttered as he pushed the door open.

The room was much larger than Sienna had

expected, with a bay window overlooking the front pond.

A beautiful Victorian dressing table sat next to the chair where Violet waited for them, watching the door. With a quick glance, Sienna's eyes widened as she spotted the open door of the closet. She blinked a few times and found herself moving closer. She hesitated at the door.

"You can look," Violet offered. "They're all mine from years gone by."

Very carefully, Sienna reached forward and pulled out a royal blue dress that had fallen to the floor. The material felt soft to the touch and made Sienna turn to Violet. "This is beautiful." She shook her head and put it back in the closet, glancing at the others.

"I think my mind is stuck in the past," Violet offered.

Sienna moved closer and scanned the black and white photographs in beautiful frames that covered the dresser, and that was all Sienna saw - her attention completely captured.

"You like my collection?" Violet asked, her gaze unmoving.

Sienna wet her lips with the tip of her tongue. "I do. Very much."

Violet didn't smile but shifted her gaze to the two

chairs that had been placed around where she was sitting. Jake pushed Sienna into one and then sat down next to her.

"Why are you here?"

Sienna looked at Jake and winced, except he gave her an encouraging smile and said, "Have you met Luke Carlisle's caregiver, Sienna?"

The old lady snapped her eyes at Sienna and stared at her as if she wanted her to burst into flames. After a few minutes, she finally smiled. "You want to know about Luke?"

"That's why we're here," Sienna informed her, leaning forward. "We wanted to know anything you could tell us about him, about his time on the Titanic and his life in New York after that. What happened to him on the ship?"

For a while, Violet sat in silence, a million thoughts running through her mind as she watched them. Tears welled up in her old eyes. Her face was wrinkled with age, but she looked as if she missed nothing. Her dress was black and styled much like the others in the closet. She dressed as if she were still on the ship.

Sienna met Violet's gaze and admitted to the elderly lady with a head full of silver hair, "Before Luke died, he became obsessed with a friend of Jake's." She glanced briefly at him, and then focused back on

Violet. "He kept telling her to, and I quote, 'come back to me', which was a strange thing to say. He gave her a locket that refused to open."

"Until the night she wore the dress Luke had given her. It opened, right before she disappeared," Jake added.

They certainly had Violet's attention now. "Disappeared?" She frowned, but a knowing look flashed across her face.

"The woman we are trying to find information on is Esmé Rogers." Jake took Sienna's hand the moment he said Esmé's name.

The woman gasped and stilled, clutching a hand to her chest. When she appeared to be struggling for breath, Sienna jumped up to assist.

Violet waved her off. "I'm fine. It was a shock hearing her name after all these years."

"You knew her?"

Violet turned her head toward the photographs on her dresser, and whispered, "She gave me the life I've lived all these years with the man I fell in love with on the Titanic. I'm ready to join him now. I have been since the day he died."

Sienna had to blink away tears, and Jake was in the same position.

"I boarded the ship as Esmé's maid. Within an

hour of knowing her, she announced we were the best of friends. I was never a maid again." She sighed and dipped her head. "Can you pass me the large wedding photograph please?"

"Yeah, sure." Jake found the one Violet meant and stood staring at the photograph before he lifted his gaze and met Sienna's. "Esmé and Luke are on here. They married on the Titanic?" He watched Violet who stared at the photograph in his hands.

"A double wedding. April 14th, 1912." Violet smiled, lost in the past. "Esmé was so in love with Luke, and he loved her with every breath in his body. When she disappeared without a trace, he changed. He wouldn't talk about her. He closed himself off from everyone."

"When did she disappear?" Sienna asked the question they wanted to know the answer to the most.

Violet asked a question of her own, "How did Luke find her?"

"It's a crazy story, if you have time?"

She laughed. "I haven't walked in a few years young man, so I don't think I'm going anywhere."

VIOLET SAT IN SILENCE, STARING AT SIENNA AND Jake. They had recounted the story from the first time Esmé had met Luke to the night she had disappeared from Jake's sight. It was an incredible story, and Sienna knew they sounded crazy, but she needed Violet to believe them.

"That explains a lot," Violet finally whispered, her hands shaking. "She was upset about something and didn't know how to tell Luke. They finally agreed to talk about what was bothering her once they arrived in New York." She held Sienna's gaze. "She would have known in advance what happened to the Titanic if she was from that year?"

"She did." Jake sat forward. "I take it she never said anything?"

Violet shook her head slowly. "Not a word, except —" her eyes fogged over and for ten minutes Violet was lost in the past. "I don't understand how it's possible to travel through time, but for what happened later, I don't think I'd believe you."

"What happened?" Sienna asked eagerly.

Violet ignored her question. "That night," she whispered, "after our wedding and dinner at the captain's table, she asked us to meet her on deck at half past eleven. She told us to wear our warmest clothes; hats, gloves, anything that would keep us warm." She wiped tears from her eyes. "We weren't too keen, and neither was Luke, since it was her wedding night."

She smiled softly and then her eyes filled with fear. "We were on deck when the Titanic hit the iceberg. You could feel the impact as it shook the whole ship."

"So, she never told anyone what was going to happen?"

"Not that I know of. She didn't even tell us, just made sure we were dressed for the cold. A while later she started a fight on a lifeboat." She sighed. "I think I need to rest now." She looked at her photos and added,

"If you two want to come back tomorrow, I'll tell you more and what happened aboard the Carpathia."

Jake laughed and Sienna looked surprised, while Violet gave them a mischievous smile, knowing she'd baited the hook. They'd be back.

"Thank you for talking to us," Sienna said as she stood up.

"We appreciate your time." Jake took Sienna's hand.

"I didn't know you knew Luke and Esmé when you came to see me."

Jake nodded and pulled Sienna out of the room.

They remained silent until they had driven a few miles from the house, and then Sienna asked, "Do you think Esmé made it to the Carpathia?"

With a heavy sigh, Jake replied, "I think she did. Violet didn't indicate otherwise, and I think she would have said if she was lost on the Titanic. As far as I know, nothing happened on the Carpathia that made it into the history books." He tapped the wheel. "Maybe we should go to the library and look through the newspaper articles from that time; see if anything pops up."

"I'd rather go home and eat," Sienna said quietly, it had been a long day and she was ready to go home.

"Besides, whatever happened, we'll know about it tomorrow. At least I hope so."

"Violet knew how to get us back to her." Jake chuckled. "Do you think she's lonely? We don't really know anything about her life."

Sienna rested her head on the seat and admired Jake in profile. He needed a shave, though she found she liked him like this - denim and plaid - handsome in a rugged sort of way. She preferred him like that, rather than in his suits, because he was much more approachable.

"A dime for your thoughts?" he asked, frowning.

When they got stuck behind a van, she reached out and gently rubbed his forehead. "I'm not thinking anything worth that frown." She smiled softly and met his gaze.

Jake slowly moved closer and then his lips brushed hers gently as he spoke, "I think too hard sometimes." His lips pressed against hers, devouring her softness.

A loud horn honked behind their car and separated them, her lips still warm and wet from his kiss as his eyes lingered on her face. Jake swallowed hard before pulling back into traffic. "Let me take you to dinner?" She gave him a quick smile. "And we'll talk about anything but Esmé and the Titanic."

"You have a deal." Sienna beamed, thrilled that Esmé wasn't the only one finding happiness.

Chapter Sixteen

April 14th, 1912

19:30

The smile on my face matched the blush on Violet's as our eyes met. Violet laughed and hugged James.

"Your friend is happy," Luke whispered into my ear with a chuckle. His lips brushed a kiss along my neck before he straightened and winked. "I know the feeling," he murmured as he turned to greet his brother.

"This is exciting," Olive gushed, pulling me into a hug. "Matthew's mother will be beside herself when we get home. I'm giving her another grandchild to adore, and Luke has given her a new daughter."

I felt like my smile was frozen. I longed for all the talk of tomorrow, but I knew what tonight would offer many of the people in the room. And I wanted to save them all. I felt heartbroken. Why had I appeared on the Titanic if I couldn't change the course of events? There had to be a reason. Not knowing frustrated me.

"I think they're ready for us in the saloon," Matthew commented, nodding in the direction of the waving purser.

"Why did we agree to this?" Luke muttered.

I smiled up at him with a twinkle in my eye. "Because we thought it would be a nice way to remember our wedding day."

"I'll remember our wedding day as long as I live." Luke quickly kissed my cheek and hovered. "I want to capture your lips with mine, but I think I'd cause too much trouble if I did that here."

I licked my lips in thought as I looked into his eyes. "I'm not sure I want you to stop."

Luke made a sound in the back of his throat before quickly taking me by the arm and marching me into the dining room, much to my amusement. "You are incorrigible, Mr. Carlisle."

He smiled. "You shouldn't be so adorable, Mrs. Carlisle."

"I see the newlyweds are punctual," the captain said. "Please be seated."

The first thing I noticed was our wedding photograph, which brought tears to my eyes. Luke kissed my cheek and, after a closer look, put it in his pocket. "I'll never lose this or forget how mesmerizing you looked in your wedding dress."

"And I won't forget how handsome my husband looked in his tuxedo."

Luke held my gaze and I blushed at the intensity of his look.

He squeezed my hand and drew my attention to the beautifully set table. A small cake sat in front of each place setting.

"Ah, you've discovered tonight's treat! I told Chef Baker to come up with something special, and he didn't disappoint."

"They're beautiful," I sighed, smiling as I overheard Violet asking James what he thought they were.

"Cake," the captain added, his lips twitching. "And here are our other guests."

I glanced over my shoulder and smiled at the approaching couple. I had no idea who they were, but I'd seen them a few times around the ship and in the saloon.

The woman, introduced by the captain as Scarlett Young, was older than me. Her beautiful blue silk dress, covered with silver beads, was stunning, and I found that I couldn't take my eyes from it. "Your dress is beautiful," I whispered, finally raising my eyes to meet Scarlett's.

"Thank you." Scarlett smiled. "My sister and I love to sew. I've discovered that our creations always attract the attention of others. I only wear our clothes now. This is one of mine."

"You're very talented," I commented.

"My wife is brilliant," Edward, her husband, added with a robust smile. "I believe congratulations are in order?" he announced.

Scarlett raised her glass. "Yes, I think we should toast the newlyweds."

"To the newlyweds," the captain toasted.

A few minutes later, I offered, "Violet is interested in the design business." I grinned at Violet and gave her hand a quick squeeze.

"My wife can do anything her heart desires when we get to New York," James said gruffly. "Even learn how to make wonderful, eye-catching dresses."

Violet blushed, but I didn't miss the love shining in her fierce gaze for her new husband.

"Thank you," she said, holding his hand.

Luke caught my attention. "Are you well?" he whispered into my ear, sending shards of pleasure down my spine.

My lips brushed against his as I turned to face him. "Everything is perfect."

I caught John trying to get my attention from the entrance to the dining room. I guessed from his actions that he wanted me to meet him after dinner.

Even the breath of a kiss that Luke had planted on my cheek couldn't dispel the nerves that were rapidly growing in my stomach.

21:00

Luke planted a lingering kiss on my cheek before disappearing into the smoke room with his brother and James. I hadn't missed the wince he had given. He hated the smoke room, so he wouldn't be in there long.

I only half listened to Olive, Violet, and Scarlett as I excused myself, "I'll just be a moment." Olive and Scarlett smiled, and Violet frowned with a glance at the doorway where John had been before she looked back at me.

I placed a hand on the younger girl's shoulder. "It's okay."

As I moved between passengers and other tables,

my heart raced with the hope that John had found a way to at least slow down the ship. When I found him waiting for me, I knew he hadn't come up with anything. His face was downcast, and he looked disheveled.

"Nothing."

He shook his head. "I can't ask anyone, because if I did, the Master at Arms would take me away. It's serious to sabotage a ship," he whispered.

"I know, but you'd be saving lives."

"They don't know what's going to happen, and we can't tell them unless we want to disappear." He waved his arms around, agitated.

I paced in front of him. A quick glance into the dining room confirmed that Luke hadn't returned.

I paused. "I can't believe I never thought to ask this before, but do you ever make it to a lifeboat?"

He shook his head slowly, his eyes showing fear. "Every time I drown."

My heart went out to him as I noticed Luke's appearance in the dining room. I said, "I'll meet my family on deck at half past eleven. You can meet us too. We're all getting off this ship." I turned and walked toward Luke with a smile on my face.

I really hoped that John would meet us on deck

and that I would succeed in getting us all into the lifeboats. It was my only option.

"I wondered where you disappeared to," Luke commented, putting an arm around my shoulders.

"Some fresh air." I smiled, my conscience eating away at me.

Scarlett and Edward slipped away, so I turned to the others. "I know this is going to sound crazy, but please don't ask me questions I can't answer."

"What is it, Esmé? You can tell me anything." Luke brushed a lock of hair over my shoulder.

"It's not that, but I will explain, I promise." I bit my lip, thinking of my plan. "For now, I just need you to meet us on deck at half past eleven," I said hurriedly. "It's really important. Dress warmly."

They stared at me but nodded in agreement. "We'll be there," James said.

"I'm curious, so we'll join you," Matthew added.

I turned to Luke. "Can we go back to our room?"

"Of course." He offered a wry smile, a hand slipping to my waist.

22:00

"I love you," Luke said as soon as the door to our

cabin closed. "I am very curious, but I trust you will tell me what is going on when we get to New York."

I wrapped my arms around my husband's waist and felt Luke rest his chin on the top of my head. "Thank you. I want to tell you now, but I can't for reasons I can't tell you. I will explain everything, I promise. I know I'm being cryptic, but it's a great relief that you trust me."

He kissed the top of my head while holding me close to his chest. We stayed like that until Luke gently cupped my chin and raised my face to his.

Love was reflected in his gaze as he lowered his face to mine, his tongue tracing the soft fullness of my lips, sending shivers of desire through me. He lifted his mouth from mine, his lips wet - his eyes full of desire. "I love you, Esmé," his words were smothered on my lips.

I tangled my fingers in Luke's hair and held him close. I shivered as Luke ran his hands over my waist and hips, finally unfastening my dress and letting it fall to the floor. "Exquisite," Luke whispered, his hands shaking.

Unable to wait any longer, I reached out and quickly helped Luke free himself from the confines of his clothing. My body was overwhelmed with desire. Before Luke could see me blush with embarrassment,

I buried my face in his chest and wrapped my arms around his waist. My breasts tingled against his hairy chest. Luke let out a loud moan and shivered in against me.

"I need you," I confessed. "I need you right now." I tilted my face up to Luke's.

He swallowed hard and gently laid me down on the bed. I gasped at the sensation of his body over mine, his penis thick and heavy. His lips brushed over my nipples as I lay panting beneath him, my chest heaving. I writhed beneath him, eager for more.

His fingers burned against my tingling skin as they slid across my silken belly and moved down, skimming both sides of my body to my thighs. One of his hands slid to my bottom as I wrapped a hand around the warmth of his arousal.

"You feel like silk," I whispered in wonder. "But hard as steel."

Luke groaned, his hand lightly touching my hardened nipples before he dipped his head and took one into his mouth. I rose to meet him in a moment of uncontrolled passion. He slipped into my welcoming warmth, a shiver of ecstasy running through both of us. My body melted against his and the world filled with nothing but Luke – my husband.

His touch was divine ecstasy and my hands

reached for him, caressing the length of his back before massaging the tendons in his neck. Flames of passion burned in both of us. His breathing was labored as I felt sweet agony before waves of ecstasy pounded through us, shattering us into a million glowing stars.

Luke wrapped me in his embrace and rolled me onto my side, his weight crushing me. Satisfaction and peace flowed between us as Luke took a lock of my hair and gently caressed it between his thumb and finger.

"I love you with everything in me," I whispered, succumbing to the numbed sleep of a contented lover.

23:30

It was cold on deck as I rubbed my hands together for warmth. Luke covered them with his big hands and blew warm air onto them. "I hadn't realized how cold it was on deck this late at night." Luke paused. "The bed will keep us nice and warm," he whispered for my ears only.

I blushed slightly before giving him a dazzling smile.

"Damn, it's so cold," Violet complained, James' arm around her shoulders.

"You could say that," Matthew added, glancing at me before a crewman caught his eye. He nodded at the man. "He probably thinks we're all crazy to be out here at this hour."

I winced. After all, I knew what was about to happen and they didn't. I grew more and more uncomfortable by the second as my dismay grew. Uncertainty crept into Luke's face as I remained silent and watched him. What could I say? There was nothing that would reassure him. And in a few moments, it would be a race against time to get us safely off the ship. Especially since I knew that the captain would order the women and children to leave first.

"Esmé?" Luke asked.

My mind was filled with doubt and fear as my eyes met my husband's. When I tried to speak, my voice wavered, and I closed my mouth.

Luke reached up and caressed my face before resting his forehead against mine. "I trust you."

Before I had a chance to answer, John ran up to me.

I turned quickly and met his worried gaze. "Now." As soon as John uttered the word, the whole world seemed to go silent.

"What's going on?" Matthew muttered, moving

closer to the side of the ship to see what the crew was looking at.

James followed, his hand clasped tightly around Violet's, as if he didn't want her anywhere but at his side.

I clasped Luke's hand and slowly looked up, fear knotting inside me as I caught my first glimpse of the iceberg. It looked over a hundred feet tall, rising out of the ocean.

James, Violet, and Matthew moved quickly back, their feet thundering on the deck along with those of the panicked crew. Matthew wrapped Olive in his arms and held her close to his chest.

A handful of passengers were nearby, and they seemed frozen.

Overwhelming fear raced through me as I watched the disaster unfold before my eyes.

Luke wrapped his arms around my middle from behind and moved quickly away from the iceberg.

"We have to get below," he shouted.

His words broke through my fear. "No!" I panicked. "We can't go below."

Suddenly, chunks of ice landed on the deck to the sound of gasps and screams. The sound of the iceberg cutting into the Titanic's hull was something I would never forget. The loud groan was like a leviathan rising from the murky depths - the ship screaming in pain and fear. It was terrifying, and I wanted to run, but we had nowhere to go. "It's damaging the ship," James said in disbelief. "Sounds like it's cutting her open."

He didn't know how accurate that description was.

I turned my terrified gaze to Luke, whose face had gone white. "You knew this would happen?"

Tears quivered on my eyelids as I nodded slowly. "I can't say any more. I desperately want to, but I can't." Tears trickled down my cheeks.

"Esmé?" my name was called in a hurry, filled with impatience.

I turned in the circle of Luke's arms, having forgotten about John, which didn't sit well with me.

"You know what to do," he said, turning away.

I reached out and grabbed his arm. "What do I do?"

John paused. "Find a boat that will take men." He ran off.

"What did he mean?" Olive whispered, confused as she clung to Matthew, her face filled with fear.

The other two couples moved closer, so I admitted in a fearful voice, "There aren't enough lifeboats for everyone." I inhaled and held Luke's gaze. "The usual rule of women and children first will apply, of course.

There will be no boats for the men." Fear, stark and vivid, flickered in my eyes.

Luke forced a smile and caressed my cold cheek with a finger. "I love you." He tugged a loose lock of hair behind her ear. "So much, Esmé." Tears welled in his eyes.

Smothering a sob, I threw myself into his arms. "I will not leave you." Tears clogged my throat. "Do you hear me? We go together," I cried.

24:45

TIME PASSED QUICKLY AS THE PANIC AND CONFUSION grew. It didn't take long for the passengers to realize that the ship was doomed.

In a panic, people surrounded the first lifeboat to be loaded, some hesitating, not really believing it was necessary to get in. Eventually it was slowly lowered, half empty, into the ocean below. Others grumbled and tried to push their way to the next lifeboat.

I wished with all my heart that I didn't know the outcome. There was an ice-cold ball of fear in my stomach that I wouldn't be able to save my family and, most importantly, the man I loved. *Luke had survived though!*

"We have to find a lifeboat. Get the women off," Matthew said, a hint of fear in his voice as he searched his wife's face.

Luke tightened his arms around me as a wave of loss suddenly washed over me. Tears stung my eyes as relentlessly as the cold night air. "I will not leave this ship unless Luke is with me."

"Esmé," Luke said quietly. He turned me to face him. "I want to know you're safe." He kissed my forehead. "I need you to be safe."

I reached up and cupped Luke's beautiful face. "That's what I need for you, too. Please don't ask me to leave without you."

He sighed heavily and pulled me to his chest.

"I agree with Esmé. We all go, or we all stay," Violet said, her lips quivering.

"No," Matthew disagreed. "Olive is pregnant and has to get off this boat with or without me."

Olive burst into tears and buried her face in Matthew's chest. Matthew rested his chin on the top of her head, tears streaming down his face.

It was obvious to me that Olive and Matthew had to get off the boat first, but how was the biggest dilemma. I had to try and save them, even though I knew their fate.

With the orchestra playing in the background, I remained silent, thinking. I couldn't concentrate because all my thoughts were on the man whose arms held me tightly against him.

With a sudden surge of fear, I pulled away from Luke. "Follow me."

Luke grabbed my hand and held it tightly as I pushed and shoved my way through the desperate passengers.

Another lifeboat had female passengers and children on board, but it was far from full.

"Wait!" I shouted.

"Get in, Miss. Hurry!"

I pushed Olive closer. "You have to save her. She's pregnant, and her husband must go with her."

The crewman on the lifeboat shook his head. "No men. Captain's orders."

I had a thought as I looked at the others in the lifeboat. "Who will row once in the water?"

The startled crewman looked around. I continued, "Matthew is stronger than anyone in the boat. He can row you quickly to a safe distance. I promise. You need him."

The crewman looked around nervously. "Quickly. Now!"

"Esmé, I can't take the place of another woman or child," Matthew said, his eyes drifting to the boat.

"Listen to me. The boat is leaving and there is room for at least twenty more people. Go with Olive. We'll find another one. He won't take us all."

"Brother, go," Luke urged before pulling him into a hug. "I love you."

"I love you too," Matthew whispered, choking back tears.

Once aboard, myself, Luke, Violet, and James watched until Olive and Matthew were free of the ship.

"We have to find other boats and use the same excuse I used for Matthew." I faced Luke. "You and James are big, strong men. You'll have more strength to row than the young crewmen in the boats."

"I hope you're right. You must promise me that you'll go regardless of whether I'm on the boat with you," Luke begged.

My eyes filled with tears. "I can't make that promise. I love you. I refuse to leave without you."

"I love you too." Luke put an arm around her shoulders. "Let's find a less crowded place to think."

We moved to where the first lifeboat had been launched, the area now deserted.

"I think we should do what Esmé suggested," James said. "It worked for Matthew."

Would they be so lucky next time? More passengers panicked now.

01:40

"Over there," Luke called, dragging me in his wake as Violet and James followed.

"What is it?" I had begun to panic, knowing we had less than an hour to get to safety. There was already a tilt to the port side of the ship.

A lifeboat with about ten passengers on board had started to leave. Ridiculous!

"Please can we get in?" Luke begged.

The crewman ignored him or didn't hear him over the noise.

"Please," I pleaded. "Our husbands can row us away from the ship quickly, otherwise, if the ship sinks, we'll be pulled down with it if we're too close."

The crewman raised his head. I gasped. "John?"

"I've been looking for you," he said, as if he couldn't believe I was standing in front of him. "Get aboard, all of you. Quickly!"

After a shocked pause, I led the way into the lifeboat.

"John?" I asked again.

He shook his head and climbed up, fumbling with the rope. Before I could say anything, the boat was lowered. It felt like an eternity before the boat finally bobbed on the ocean, but it was only moments.

Luke and James helped John free the boat before quickly grabbing an oar and rowing us away from the rapidly sinking ship.

I felt numb. John should have been with me, but he'd been lost in the crowd. And my thoughts had been on saving everyone I loved. But questions swirled around me, and I needed answers. Only I couldn't ask them in front of all the passengers. John knew. "I didn't want to go in the water this time," he said, holding my gaze.

"I understand." I dabbed at a tear. "Thank you."

John nodded. "Miss."

Violet huddled against me. "I'm bundled up, but it's so cold."

"We'll be warm and dry soon," I reasoned. "Then we'll all meet up with Olive and Matthew and swap stories." I hoped that would be the case - I hoped desperately.

The silence of the ocean became frightening as we

moved away from the Titanic. The dark night surrounded us, with only the lights of the ship illuminating the horizon. The cold seeped through my clothes, and I couldn't stop shivering. When I breathed, it left a trail of fog. I clung to the hope that our rescue would come swiftly, imagining the relief of being wrapped in a warm blanket and sipping hot tea.

When we were at a safe distance from the Titanic, the lifeboat stopped. "We're going back to help find survivors after the ship sinks," Luke announced.

Luke's words filled me with a mixture of admiration and fear. As we turned back towards the sinking ship, I wondered if we were putting our own lives at risk. The thought of facing the icy waters again sent a shiver down my spine, but I knew that the bravery and determination of those on board the lifeboat could make a difference in saving more lives.

"I don't think that's such a good idea. Certainly not safe for us," a woman in the back of the boat disagreed.

"If you survived the sinking, wouldn't you want to be helped?" I snapped.

Silence followed.

We watched in stunned disbelief as the huge ship slowly began to disappear.

Then the lights went out.

02:18

To our astonishment, the Titanic suddenly broke in two. The sound was nothing compared to the shouts and screams coming from the ship that chilled me to the bone.

I placed a hand to my mouth as tears streamed down my face. Nothing had prepared me for the horror of witnessing such tragedy.

"Oh, my God," Violet gasped. "Those poor people."

"Should we go back now?" James asked.

Both myself and John shouted, "No!"

I realized I'd lost it. "We have to wait, or we will be pulled in after the ship."

Luke wrapped his hand around mine and held on tightly.

02:20

With a loud groan, the Titanic began to rise slowly into the night. Screams filled the air as people slipped and fell to their deaths in the icy water.

The stern hung there, frozen in the cold air, before it slid silently into the ocean and disappeared from sight, leaving an eerie silence.

"We should go back now," Luke suggested quietly. "We have to be careful. We don't want to be rushed, or they'll capsize the lifeboat." He squeezed my hand.

There was nervous movement in the boat at the suggestion. It soon subsided as Luke and James rowed back towards where the ship had disappeared beneath the icy waters. Wreckage was everywhere, along with some dead - many of them frozen.

Pain clutched at my heart at what I had just witnessed, although I felt relief that my husband and others had survived. I didn't find the thought cruel, more like human nature.

The search took a long time, but a few other boats could be seen in the distance. Their searchlights lit a path through the murky surface.

"I think that's it," John looked out, but there was no sound. He turned to the others. "Let's get away from here. Not too far, we don't want the rescue boats to miss us."

After pulling five passengers from the water, it took another thirty minutes to clear the lifeboat of debris.

Luke wrapped himself gently around me, his face nuzzling into my neck.

No words were necessary as the despair around us spoke for itself.

My eyes locked with John's, and I knew without a doubt that he'd saved my life and that of my family. I murmured, "Thank you."

He tilted his head to the side. "My future is unknown now."

I reached out and took his hand. "We'll all stay together, John."

"I hope so, Miss."

Nestled in Luke's arms, I felt safe. And I believed that now the disaster was over, we might have the chance to grow old together.

I hoped, at least.

03:10

I had never felt seasick before, but after several hours in the lifeboat, my stomach was queasy.

Luke's arms held me close, even though his back must have been aching from sitting in the same position.

I looked at Violet and smiled because my friend looked tiny with the way James was protecting her from the elements.

"We'll be rescued by morning," Luke said confidently. "Or maybe sooner," his voice trailed off.

228

I turned my head and followed Luke's gaze to the distant horizon.

The Carpathia.

"Is that a ship, Ma?" a small child asked.

"I hope so."

The child stared at Luke. "You were right," she said.

Luke grinned. "I always am."

I laughed. "What's your name?" I asked the child.

"Lottie Sarah McCormick," she told me proudly, giving her mother a smug grin.

Her mother chuckled, a welcome sound after the horrors of the night. "Charlotte Sarah McCormick. We're from Delgany, County Wicklow. My husband awaits us in New York." Her lip wobbled. "He'll be so worried when he hears about the ship." She shook her head. "He worked and saved to get us second-class passage."

"Don't cry, Ma. We'll still get to Pa. You always tell me to have faith."

She smiled through her tears. "I'm Sarah, and as you already know, this is my daughter. She's an eight-year-old handful."

The passengers on the boat shared their names, but Lottie, who obviously preferred this to Charlotte, was the most entertaining now that she had her second wind.

Question after question.

I felt sorry for the child's mother. "Lottie, tell me, what are you going to do in New York?"

Lottie's red curls danced down her back as she became animated. "I'm going to eat a lot of ice cream and try lots of Italian food with my Pa. He promised to show Ma and me all the sights in New York. But I'm going to have my own adventure to tell him about now."

"You will," I agreed. "You have such beautiful hair."

"She gets it from her Pa's side of the family," Sarah added.

"The ship is getting closer," James announced, drawing my gaze towards the Carpathia.

My stomach fluttered with nerves, and for once I felt more confident that I would have a future with Luke.

07:22

We dozed on and off, but sleep wouldn't really come until we were out of the lifeboat, which would be soon.

The Carpathia was perhaps twenty feet from us as we waited to be called closer to the ship.

I would be thrilled if I wasn't so tired.

It took another twenty minutes to get us aboard. I almost fell, my legs weak from the cold and from sitting in the same position for hours.

"I've got you." Luke put an arm around my waist.

Two women on the Carpathia wrapped a blanket around each of us. "Please follow me," one woman said.

"Violet and James?" I asked, coming to a halt.

"Your friends are being looked after," she smiled. "I'm Josephine, and I'll take you both to my cabin." She paused. "You are married?"

"Yes," Luke replied.

Josephine smiled and continued down the passage. I exchanged a quick glance with Luke.

"Thank you for your help," Luke added. "I just want to keep my wife warm."

"May I take your names?" a crewman asked.

"Luke Carlisle and Esmé Carlisle," Luke informed him.

I frowned. If my name had been given, why hadn't I found it on the list of survivors when I had researched in New York? Surely, I would have seen my name with Luke's.

"Thank you, sir." The crewman ran off.

"This way," Josephine muttered.

Overwhelmed with relief, I was on the verge of collapse as we followed the kind woman into her cabin.

"I have put all my belongings in my sister's cabin. So please consider this yours until we arrive in New York. Tea and sandwiches will be here—" A knock interrupted her.

"Oh, here they are." She placed the tray on the table. "If you need anything, please let me know. I'm right across the hall."

"I don't know what to say," I whispered, my voice breaking.

"No need for words." Josephine smiled and left quickly.

The room was small, and the bed was a little wider than a single bed, but not by much.

"She was so kind."

"Yes." Luke sat me down on the bed. "Let me pour us some tea and we need to eat after everything."

"Okay. We also need to look for Olive and Matthew," I commented.

"They're still bringing passengers aboard, so we'll wait for now. I am no good to anyone exhausted." He looked at the bed, then at the floor.

I offered a small smile. "We'll fit in the bed. "

"That's good because I need to hold you." He yawned before finishing his tea in a few gulps. "I didn't realize I was so thirsty."

"The tea is welcome." I smiled and set down the cup.

"I'd like you to hold me on the bed while we sleep." I kicked off my boots and removed my coat. Luke did the same, leaving his pants and undershirt on.

Minutes later, we were huddled on the bed, arms wrapped tightly around each other, legs intertwined.

"I feel like I can finally breathe again. Now I know we are safe."

"I love you, Esmé. I am grateful for many things, but not as much as I am that you are safe here, in my arms, in my life."

I crawled closer and buried my face in his neck. "I want to spend the rest of my life in your arms, Luke."

We clung to each other until sleep claimed us.

11:30

I hugged Violet so tightly that I finally had to release my hold so that my friend could breathe. "I'm so happy we're together." I pulled back. "We have to find Olive and Matthew." I bit my lip anxiously.

"All the names have been taken, so that might be a place to start," James offered.

"You're right," Luke said wearily.

I knew my husband was worried, and I hoped they were alive and well on the Carpathia.

"I'll go and see," Luke said.

"Not on your own." I slipped my hands through his and clasped his arm.

Luke patted my hand and said to the other couple, "We'll meet you back here in, say, thirty minutes."

"Okay, Luke," James agreed, a frown creasing his forehead.

Violet squeezed my hand as Luke led me away to find his brother.

In the end, I wished we hadn't moved from the room we had been given, because we couldn't find Matthew and Olive on any lists.

I gripped Luke's hand tightly and asked the question Luke couldn't get out. "Are these complete?"

"Yes, Miss."

"So, every single passenger who came aboard is on these? Correct? They were on a lifeboat."

The crewman lowered his eyes and said, "A few lifeboats capsized before we arrived in the area. We were careful not to miss anyone. Everyone should be on the list unless they deliberately avoided us."

My eyes filled with tears.

"I am sorry for your loss." The man moved away.

"William?" Luke's voice broke as he sobbed his nephew's name.

I slowly led my husband to a more secluded corner. My arms wrapped around his middle as I held him close. "I'm so sorry."

He said nothing, only tightened his grip on me. Then I felt him tremble against me as the tears finally broke free.

I held him until he calmed, then watched as he wiped his face with a clean handkerchief.

"I'm—"

"No," I said quickly, knowing what he was about to say. "I know you, and you will not apologize for your grief." I reached up and cupped his face before kissing his lips. "I am your wife and I love you very much. We will make sure that William is always reminded of his parents. We will love him as our own." I smiled through my tears.

Luke inhaled, his eyes moist. "I think I'd better go back to our room. I need to be alone."

I tried to hide the hurt his words caused, but Luke caught it. "I'm sorry, I meant with you. I don't feel like being social." He glanced around before meeting my gaze. "I just want to be alone with you while I try to process what happened."

I understood. "I'll meet you there. Let me go and tell Violet and James first."

"I should come with you."

"No. I'll be fine on my own." I kissed his lips quickly. "I promise to be quick."

I watched Luke walk into the cabin; his shoulders slumped in defeat. Tears hovered on my lashes as I watched him, my heart breaking.

I quickly blinked them away before heading over to meet Violet and James.

"I'M NERVOUS, JAKE."

He stopped and cupped Sienna's face. After planting a kiss on her pink lips, he smiled. "So am I, but I'm also impatient to find out what happened to Esmé. It's like a story you read quickly to find out the ending."

Sienna frowned. "I understand, but what if we don't like what Violet tells us? It's more than a story."

"You're right, as always." Jake smiled.

"I like that you think I'm always right." Sienna flirted.

Jake laughed and turned serious when he caught Violet watching them through the window. He cleared his throat. "We've been spotted." He took Sienna's hand and led her inside.

"Just remember, you're not alone," Jake whispered as he pushed open the door to Violet's room.

The older woman sat regally in her chair. The silver hair was in a neat bun at Violet's nape. Her hands were lightly clasping a white silk handkerchief.

"You look well rested," Sienna commented.

"I slept well, dreaming of my husband." She looked whimsical. "He is waiting for me, but he said I must finish my story before I can join him." A hand reached up and dabbed at her eyes.

Sienna wanted to cry her eyes out, and a glance at Jake's face told her he felt the same way.

"So let me tell you." She sighed and waited for Jake and Sienna to join her.

"It was so cold on the deck of the Titanic as we huddled together. Only Esmé seemed to know what we were waiting for. I certainly wasn't expecting the iceberg or anything that followed.

"I am not good at judging size or distance, but the iceberg was over a hundred feet high and maybe three or four hundred feet wide. I've never seen anything like it before or since." She shivered and pulled her woolen shawl around her shoulders.

"When it became clear that the ship was sinking, there was panic. Esmé got us all to find lifeboats. She convinced them to let the men on board so they could man the oars. It wasn't difficult when the lifeboat we arrived at was being steered by John, a crewman who happened to be a friend of Esmé's. He told us all to get in.

"In the end, it was James and Luke who rowed the boat to get us away from the ship."

"Were Olive and Matthew with you?" Sienna asked, wanting to know what had happened to William's parents.

Violet shook her head. "Olive was pregnant, so Esmé argued with a crewman, and he let them on board one of the first lifeboats. It would have been too much begging for all of us, so we found the one John had control of.

"In retrospect, I wish we had waited, and all got on the same lifeboat, because the one Olive and Matthew were on capsized. Neither of them could swim. We didn't discover this until we'd been on the Carpathia for some time.

"Esmé blamed herself for forcing them into the boat. She hadn't, and Luke told her so. They were grief-stricken. We all were.

"James took care of me and then, days later, we

arrived in New York, which was overwhelming." Violet hesitated before continuing.

"In New York, a couple we had met at our wedding dinner, Scarlett and Edward, became close friends of ours. Scarlett was a special friend. Between her and her sister Martha, I learned to design and sew ladies' evening gowns.

"Our store was popular for a long time. We survived wars and depressions. Everything the economy could throw at us. But eventually we got too old to keep up with the demand and sold the store."

As the silence continued with Violet lost in thought, Jake asked, "What happened to Luke and Esmé?"

"Luke, I can tell you, but Esmé? I have no idea." She put the handkerchief over her mouth and swallowed a few times.

"Luke became a recluse. He worked, but his heart was broken, and no one could mend it. You see, his wife, my beautiful friend Esmé, disappeared aboard the Carpathia as we sailed into New York."

"What?" Sienna gasped.

"No!" Jake hissed.

Jake was as invested in the story as Sienna was, and he'd been praying that Esmé had stayed with the man she loved. His own heart was slowly being repaired by

Sienna and he cared enough about Esmé to want her to have the love she deserved.

"How? What happened?" Sienna asked.

"One minute she was there, and then she wasn't. The ship was searched, but there was no sign of her. The conclusion was that she had fallen overboard, and no one had noticed. Luke didn't believe that because she had been with him and had only been out of his sight for five minutes. No one knew where she'd gone. He searched for a long time."

"That's not true."

All eyes turned to the woman at the door. She looked younger than Violet, but not by much.

"It was all my fault and I never told anyone." Her body shook as she entered the room.

20:00

THE LIGHTS OF THE SCOUT CRUISER USS CHESTER escorted the Carpathia into New York Harbor, leaving me lost in thought. I fingered the letter in my pocket and pondered the wisdom of my words to Luke.

"There's my wife." Luke's sudden interruption was welcomed as his arms wrapped around my midsection. "What do you think of New York?" he asked, then added, "Too bad we arrived in the evening."

I gripped Luke's hands. "It's a magnificent sight." I didn't admit that I hadn't noticed it before.

"I'm not sure what the house will be like once I've

told my parents and William about my brother," his voice trailed off, "and Olive."

"If you're worried about me, don't be. I will be there for you and them. Always, Luke." I turned in his arms.

"What would I do without you?" He kissed my lips with a soft brush of his hand before resting his chin on the top of my head.

I pressed my face against the corded muscles of his chest, savoring the moment. As I inhaled deeply, his scent filled my senses. This moment would stay with me forever, no matter where the future took us.

"I'm scared, Luke," I admitted suddenly, raising my face to his. "I have this bad feeling in the pit of my stomach."

"Oh, honey." Luke cupped my face. "What are you afraid of?"

I moaned. "Losing you." In one fluid motion, I wrapped my arms around his neck and searched for his lips.

Luke moaned, his mouth hungrily covering mine, my lips burning with fire.

A throat cleared.

Slowly breaking the kiss, Luke gazed into my eyes.

Overwhelmed with love for my husband, I buried my face in his neck, my heart racing as fast as Luke's.

"I thought it best to interrupt," James said, amused when I caught a glimpse of him.

I laughed and quickly kissed Luke on the lips. "I love you," I said before looking at Violet.

"Esmé?" Lottie shouted.

I smiled and waved at the eight-year-old. "I'll be right back," I whispered to Luke, brushing my lips against his ear.

Lottie had become a mischievous child on the ship, but everyone loved her. Around the corner from the deck and out of sight of the other passengers, I found the young child in the stairwell.

"Mama says we're leaving soon. Will I see you again?"

"I'll make sure to give you Luke's address before we leave the ship. I promise."

Lottie sulked, "I'll miss you."

I held out my arms to the child and smiled as Lottie jumped into them and clung to me.

"I will miss you very much, Charlotte," I admitted.

"Lottie!"

"I have to go," Lottie panicked at the sound of her mother's voice.

Lottie started to pull away and cried, "Ouch!" reaching for her head.

I heard a low hum. It reminded me of when I was

in my apartment in New York just before I disappeared.

That couldn't be right?

The buzzing grew louder.

My head began to spin.

With fear in my eyes, I looked at Lottie, who had the look of frozen terror on her young face.

My vision began to blur.

I was leaving.

No! Not now!

My hand reached into my coat pocket and quickly pulled out the letter I hadn't realized I would need so soon. I tossed it to Lottie and pleaded, "Please give this to Luke." My eyes pleaded before everything went black.

JAKE HELPED THE ELDERLY LADY INTO A CHAIR NEXT to Violet as they watched her quietly. She held Violet's gaze for a few moments.

"My name is Charlotte Sarah McCormick, and I was eight years old when I met Esmé and Violet in a lifeboat after the Titanic sank." Her eyes watered.

Sienna slipped her hand into Jake's. He looked at her and she gave him a small smile. "I'm okay." She turned her attention to Charlotte. "Please continue."

"Esmé gave me attention. She played games with me to let my mother rest." She smiled. "My mother was very seasick, especially after the ship sank.

"Esmé was my friend, and in the end, it had taken me ten years to fulfill her last wish.

"You see, when we were on our way to New York Harbor, she came to talk to me after I called her. I threw myself into her arms, thinking I'd never see her again.

"When I was a child, I had a head of red curls, and one of them got tangled in the chain around Esmé's neck." Charlotte paused, distress in her voice.

"Would you like a glass of water?" Sienna asked, already pouring it.

Charlotte took the glass and placed it on the table next to her.

"Not only did the chain snap, but the locket fell to the floor and snapped open.

"It was like magic. One minute everything was perfect, and the next, Esmé was blurred.

"I will never forget the look on her face as she began to fade from my vision. It was pure fear. She threw me a letter, begging me to give it to Luke. Then she was gone, and I was left holding the chain. I was terrified by what I'd seen. When I recovered from the incredible shock, I picked up the letter and the locket. For some reason I shoved the letter into my pocket. My mother found me in tears holding the locket.

"She screamed at me and only stopped when Luke appeared and took the locket and chain from me. He wanted to know where Esmé was, and I told him I found the necklace on the floor. I was afraid I was going to get in a lot of trouble because I didn't think anyone would believe what I had seen.

"Esmé was never found, as far as I know, and it wasn't until we moved when I was eighteen that I found the letter Esmé had thrown to me ten years earlier.

"Finding the letter was a shock." She took a deep breath as if to steady herself. "I'm not proud of what I did. I opened the letter and read it. When I finished, my face was drenched with tears.

"I knew what I had to do, what I should have done on the deck of the Carpathia. It took me a week, but I found Luke and put the letter through his door. I didn't stay. I was too ashamed to keep such a heartfelt letter from him for so long."

A stunned silence fell over the room, broken only by Violet's whisper, "What did the letter say?"

Slowly, with trembling hands, Charlotte took a slightly browned piece of paper from her pocket. "I copied it before I gave it to Luke."

Jake cleared his throat and took the letter. "I'm not sure how I feel about reading this, although I am curious."

"Once you read it, you'll never be able to forget the words," Charlotte said before turning to Violet.

"We've been friends for years. I hope you can forgive me for waiting ten years to give this letter to Luke."

Violet stared. "I understand, Charlotte. You were a frightened child then. I won't hold that against you. Besides, you did the right thing in the end."

Jake looked at Sienna, who nodded. "Go ahead."

April 17th, 1912

My Dearest Luke,

If you are reading this letter, I have disappeared without a trace.

Please believe me when I say that I would have moved heaven and earth to stay with you. To stay where my heart is. Unfortunately, accidents happen, and that is the only explanation for why I disappeared as suddenly as I appeared. I would never have willingly done anything to take me away from you.

As strange as it sounds, we first met in an Italian restaurant in New York in 1987. Yes, in the future, my love. That is how I knew what would happen to the Titanic and all those people on board. The wreck was discovered twelve and a half thousand feet under the ocean in September 1985. The Carpathia rescued seven hundred and five passengers and crew, but more than fifteen hundred died.

After we were rescued and safe aboard the Carpathia, I began to believe that our future had changed. Now we both know it hadn't and that I was dreaming.

I love you with every breath in my body and soul and will count the moments until we are together again.

All my love,

Forever your wife,

Esmé.

Five minutes later Jake said, "At the bottom of the letter it says page one of three. He frowned and then turned to Sienna, who was sitting next to him, her heart breaking before his eyes. He put an arm around her shoulders.

"So where did Esmé go?" Sienna asked.

"That's a good question," Violet whispered, not

really concentrating. "And why do we only have one side?"

"I didn't copy the other two pages. It was a list of things for Luke to do to get them back together," Charlotte admitted. "It was also another explanation of why she couldn't tell him before the Titanic disaster. She also told him about herself and her life in her New York.

"I wanted to copy all her instructions, but I didn't want to risk it being found by someone else. It was risky enough with the letter."

Jake and Sienna didn't know what to say.

Violet had no problem. "You both need to look for an Esmé Carlisle."

"By God!" Jake jumped up. "You're right. If she came back to another time, or even close to now, there should be something to find."

He grabbed Sienna out of the chair. "We need to go." He turned to Violet and Charlotte. "We'll be back to let you know what we find."

"Don't be too long. I'm not as young as I used to be." Violet offered a slight smile and motioned for Charlotte to stay with a wicked gleam in her eye.

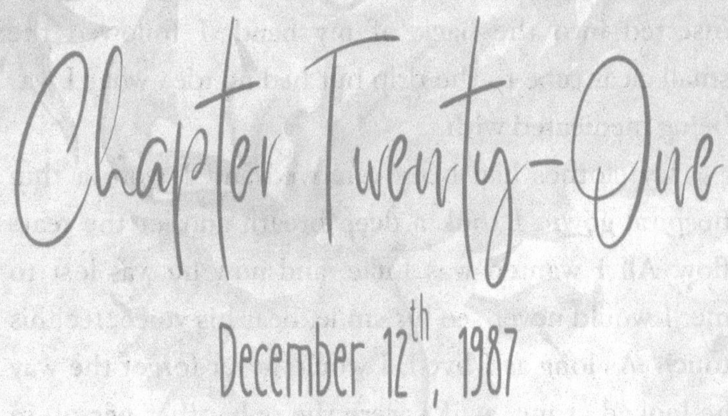

THE FOG IN MY HEAD BEGAN TO CLEAR, BUT THE voices made my heart pound. Without opening my eyes, I knew I was no longer with Luke aboard the Carpathia. A flash of wild grief tore through me, and tears seeped from under my closed lids. What would he think? Would he believe the words I had written in the letter to him? Why was I so cold?

Slowly, I opened my eyes and stared at a white, sterile wall.

Hospital?

It didn't stop the panic from rising in me as my eyes scanned the room. I desperately searched for some clue as to where I was. It slowly became clear that I was in a hospital. An intravenous cannula was inserted into the back of my hand. I followed the small clear tube to the drip but had no idea what I was being medicated with.

My clothes had been removed and I wore a thin hospital gown. I took a deep breath and let the tears flow. All I wanted was Luke, and now he was lost to me. I would never see his smile, hear his voice, feel his touch. As long as I lived, I would never forget the way he looked at me, as if I were the only other person in the world.

A nurse rushed into the room, looking as if a gust of wind would knock her over because of how petite she was. She looked at me and a look of sympathy crossed her face.

"Don't cry. It can't be all bad." The nurse grabbed some tissues and handed them to me. "I'm Colleen McCormick and I'll be your nurse during the day." She had a pleasant smile. Just hearing the name McCormick made my heart race. Her age was hard to guess, but I thought she was in her mid-fifties. Colleen had a head of thick red hair that was neatly braided down her back.

Could Colleen be related to Charlotte?

Too much of a coincidence?

While Colleen checked my pulse, I asked, "What is that liquid?"

"It's a saline solution to rehydrate you. Nothing to worry about." Colleen reassured. A frown creased her forehead as she checked all the lines and monitors. "There are two detectives outside your room who want to talk to you. One is my brother." She rolled her eyes. "He's retiring at the end of next week." She winced. "He's going to drive me crazy."

I glanced anxiously at the door. "Why? What have I done?" My voice broke at the words.

"Can you remember your name? It would be nice not to have to call you Jane Doe."

Confused, I stared at Colleen. "Why would anyone call me Jane Doe?" I rubbed my forehead. "I'm so confused."

"You were rescued from New York Harbor. You were damn lucky that worker on the docks saw you." She shook her head. "You were unconscious when they brought you in. No ID, no wallet, nothing in your pocket. You barely had a pulse, so when they brought you in, you became Jane Doe."

New York Harbor?

That was where I was when Charlotte accidentally got caught in the chain. Is that why I ended up in the harbor?

After a pause, I whispered, "Esmé Carlisle."

Colleen smiled broadly. "What a lovely name. It's my middle name."

I blinked in surprise. "Really?"

"It's unusual, isn't it? I was born Colleen Sarah Esmé McCormick." She smiled. "I took my maiden name back when I got divorced."

My head was suddenly full of questions, but I didn't want the nurse to think I was crazy. In fact, I thought my story sounded crazy.

Colleen, unaware of my turmoil, fluffed my pillows. "I'll let the doctor know you're awake and then I'll bring you a cup of warm tea and a slice of toast."

"Thank you." I sighed. "I guess you better let the detectives in, although I don't know what they want from me."

"I think they want to know how you ended up in the harbor, since no one saw you until that worker spotted. He told the detectives how one minute there was nothing and the next minute you were there." Colleen smiled. "I admit I'm curious, but I'm not going to pressure you. Why don't you wait until you see the doctor before you talk to them?"

"I think I'd rather get it over with."

Colleen tilted her head and looked at me before agreeing. "I'll tell them to come in. I'll only give them ten minutes."

"Wait!" I suddenly had a thought. "What's the date?"

"Saturday, December 12th." Colleen hesitated. "You expected me to say that didn't you?"

"What year?" My stomach rolled with tension as I waited.

Colleen frowned and took a step closer to me. "1987."

I couldn't control the sob that escaped between my dry lips. I covered my mouth with a shaking hand. "I don't want to be here. I prayed that this was a dream. I want my husband," my voice broke miserably as I cried.

Colleen tried to comfort me as I cried until there were no tears left. "I don't know what happened, but I'll help you in any way I can. I think I'll stay while the detectives are here."

The nurse helped me to and from the bathroom. When I was back in bed, the door opened, and the detectives entered. The tall one with the close-cropped red hair edged with gray gave Colleen a sharp look that probably meant she should leave, but she held her ground and took my hand.

"She's my patient, and not well enough to be pestered with questions."

"Well, Colleen, you know me better than that," the

tall detective commented. He grinned and turned to me. "I'm Detective Niall McCormick and this is my partner, Detective Kelly Armstrong. We need to ask you a few questions."

I nodded. "My name is Esmé Carlisle, and I'm twenty-five—six. I'm twenty-six."

"Do you remember how you ended up in the harbor?" Detective Armstrong asked. "There were no boats around. No one had seen you on the docks."

"Could they have missed me?"

Detective McCormick shook his head. "Not with the clothes you were wearing. It looked like you'd been to a costume party. Not from this time."

I stared out the window. "I don't remember any of this." All I wanted to do was sleep and wake up in Luke's arms. I dabbed at a tear. "I just want to go home."

"What's your address? Is there someone who will miss you?" Detective Armstrong asked.

"My husband is—is no longer here." I turned onto my side, shutting everyone out, my grief a huge, painful knot inside.

"I think it would be best to let her rest," Colleen suggested. "You have a name and an age to work with, that should be enough for now."

I had no idea what else was said because I closed

her mind. All I wanted was my husband. It felt like only a few hours since I had last seen Luke. My memory of him was so clear as I longed to be held against his strong body. Now I had no idea how I would live the rest of my life without him.

A heaviness settled in my chest.

Chapter Twenty-Two

December 15th, 1987

FROM THE WARMTH OF COLLEEN AND NIALL'S HOME, I watched the large snowflakes fall to the ground. Colleen had driven me to the house in a large car designed for snowy conditions before turning around and heading back to work. I hadn't moved in the hour I had been there, comfortable in my surroundings. It had been a huge relief and weight off my shoulders when Colleen had offered me the guest room.

Why I hadn't contacted Jake or Sienna, I didn't know, or maybe I did. Maybe they would tell me it was all in my head and I did not want to hear that. I didn't believe it, not really. They were my only friends from before, so why haven't I contact them? It had been six months since I'd disappeared. Would they know that I had found Luke? And what about Colleen and Niall?

Colleen and Niall puzzled me because I was convinced that they were Charlotte's children. Somehow, I had ended up with them. It wasn't a common name. At least not that I thought.

My forehead pressed against the cold window, while a permanent sadness weighed heavily on my chest. Even though I had only spent a few days with Luke, I had known from the moment we met that he would be forever etched in my heart. I had never known a love like the one I shared with him, and the longing to be with him had been a constant pain since I had woken up in the hospital. I was sure my heart was broken.

My thoughts were interrupted by a male voice. "Talk to me, Esmé. I want to be your friend and help you find what you're looking for." Niall smiled as he sat down in one of the chairs.

"I wouldn't know where to start," I admitted. "Everything is a mess and there are no explanations for what I've experienced." I offered a small smile, though I suspected it didn't reach my eyes. "Would you tell me more about yourself and your parents?"

I had surprised him.

"I didn't expect you to ask that, at least about my

parents." He paused. "Perhaps if I start with my mother?"

"Very inquisitive, Detective."

He laughed.

I swallowed and asked, "Are you related to a Charlotte Sarah McCormick born in either 1903 or 1904?"

Niall stared at me, and I had the feeling he already knew something. "How do you know about Charlotte?" He frowned.

"She's your mother?" I sat forward on the cushion, waiting for his answer.

"Charlotte Sarah McCormick is my mother." He cleared his throat. "Esmé, how do you know my mother? From the orphanage? Is that why she called and told me to come to the hospital?"

"I don't know how to explain," my voice trembled, "and I don't know how I ended up here with her two children when she was the last person to see me." I stared at Niall, but I didn't really see him. In my mind I saw the child with a head full of bouncing red curls.

My lips curled into a smile. "I remember Lottie's red hair. She had so much."

"It thinned with age." He smiled fondly. "It's all gray now."

Now?

I sat forward and took Niall's hand. "You mentioned a home. Is that where Lottie is?" I inhaled. "She knew I was in the hospital?"

He nodded. "Colleen wanted to take early retirement and take care of Mom here, but in the end, Mom wanted to go to the home." He shrugged. "Mom can be forgetful and a little unsteady on her feet, but she does okay. We both visit at different times during the week, so she knows we haven't forgotten her."

He smiled and continued, "She's with a friend she's known since childhood, so she's happy. That's really all we want for her - as for the phone call, my mother has known things over the years. She's never explained, and we just grew up knowing to listen. I guess I should admit that she also made a call to Colleen to make sure my sister was your nurse.

I squeezed his hand and sat back in the window seat. "I don't know how to explain the phone calls or how your mother knew where I would be. It doesn't make sense."

Charlotte had been eight when I had disappeared, so how did she know to send her son and daughter to me?

"What are you thinking?" Niall asked.

"I'm thinking," I paused, "that I'd like to visit your

mother." I held his gaze. "This may come as a shock, but I need to know how she knew to call you and Colleen."

"I'm more than curious about that, too. Why would it be a shock?" He sat forward, his elbows on his knees, his face deep with concern.

My eyes begged him to understand. "If I tell you now, you'll think I'm crazy and should be in a mental hospital, not visiting your mother." I winced. "But I promise that if you take me to Lottie, she will hopefully remember me, which will make my story less crazy." I grinned. "Or you'll just think your mom is as crazy as me."

Niall paused and then started to laugh. "I have to see this." He pulled me out of the chair and into the hallway. "Here," he said as he placed a brown woolen hat on my head. "You'll need this." He checked my feet. "You already have boots on," he observed. He held out a thick black jacket for me to slip my arms into. "I'm sure Colleen won't mind if you borrow this."

A gust of cold wind and snow blew in the moment he opened the front door. He turned and took my arm. "Are you sure about this?"

"I think I should ask if you're okay to drive in this?"

"I'll get us there. It's not far."

"Then I want to visit my friend." I smiled. Finally, I could focus on something other than despair - a way to be close to Luke.

Chapter Twenty-Three

December 15th, 1987

THE RESIDENTIAL HOME WAS A LARGE, LOW-SLUNG building built in an L-shape. Tall wrought-iron lamps lined the path leading to the main entrance. Snow had covered the ground and the building. As I turned to look out over the parking lot, I looked out over the flat land. Farmland? It was freezing outside, but the air was crisp and fresh.

"You're going to be a snowman," Niall said, pulling me inside.

We stamped our feet on the rough mats just inside the door. Niall hung up our coats and then led me to the registration desk. While he made small talk with the receptionist, I glanced around the quiet area. It was comfortable, with comfortable couches and chairs for visitors. A tall green planter decorated with gold Christmas lights sat in the corner by the window, and a red and gold poinsettia sat on the coffee table with a selection of magazines.

"This way."

I followed Niall down a large hallway that reminded me of a hospital - almost clinical. When Niall stopped in front of a closed door, he turned to me. "How big a shock?"

The nervousness in my stomach felt like it was about to explode as I met Niall's gaze. "Hopefully not too big," I chewed her lower lip, "but I'm not sure."

Niall nodded and hesitantly started to open the door to his mother's room. "When were you friends with her?"

At my first look at Charlotte, my Lottie, in over seventy years, I replied to Niall, "April 1912," while keeping my eyes on Charlotte.

The older woman slowly turned from the comfortable chair where she'd been looking out the window - a thick blanket over her legs and a knitted shawl around her shoulders.

When I got a full view of the woman's face, the image of Lottie as the mischievous child was all I saw. Overwhelmed with emotion, I swallowed hard, hot tears streaming down my face.

"Is it you?" Charlotte whispered; her eyes clouded with tears.

I nodded and took the seat Niall had pushed me into, facing his mother. "You recognize, Esmé?"

His mother smiled and dabbed at her eyes with a handkerchief. "Yes," she replied, starting to laugh. "I haven't seen her for a long time," her voice softened, "but she's exactly the same as she was when we first met." She sighed. "I'm not though."

"Mom, can you explain the phone calls to Colleen and me when Esmé was in the hospital? How did you know?"

Charlotte smiled softly. "I just knew that she needed both of you and that you would bring her to me. I prayed that Esmé would remember me and recognize your names. I especially told Colleen to make sure she gave Esmé her full name. I needed Esmé to be led back to me without saying so directly."

Niall rubbed his forehead. "You both have me confused, and that usually takes a lot." Niall settled down. "Please explain how you know each other." He looked at me.

I gave him a wry smile. "We met in a lifeboat on April 15th, 1912, watching the Titanic sink." I inhaled. "I can't explain why I was there, or how it was even possible. But I was there. Charlotte was eight years old."

Charlotte nodded slightly. "And it was my fault that Luke spent those years alone. I know that."

Charlotte's distress was real, so I quickly move and knelt at her feet. I took Charlotte's frail hands in mine. "It was an accident, Charlotte. I know that. If it hadn't happened when it did, it would have happened some other time."

"I never thought I'd see you again."

"Will you tell me what happened after I left? Did you give Luke the letter? I mean, I assume you did, because he did everything I asked."

I dropped to my knees and curled my legs under me. I followed Charlotte's eyes to Niall. Charlotte said to him, "I told you about Esmé a long time ago. I don't think I mentioned her name, but I told you about the lady who disappeared on the Carpathian."

His eyes widened, moving quickly between his mother and me. "Esmé?" He frowned. "You used to tell Colleen and me that story a lot when we were kids." He shook his head. "Are you telling me it was a true story, and the woman is Esmé? Is that what you're saying? You know how that sounds, right?"

Charlotte chuckled. "Esmé Carlisle." She sighed

and said to me, "I'll tell you what happened, but then you have to do something for me."

"I will do anything if you tell me about Luke," I pleaded, my heart in my throat.

Sitting back in the chair, Charlotte looked out the window and remained silent. Niall helped me up and pointed to the chair he'd been sitting in. "Sit down." He smiled and handed me a glass of water and put another on the table for his mother.

"I was always full of energy. My mother told me I was moving even when I slept." Charlotte began her story slowly, her voice growing stronger as she got lost in the past. "We had almost docked in New York, and I remember being afraid I'd never see you again. You pulled me into your arms, and then I heard my mother calling. She used the tone of voice that told me I was in trouble." She smiled through the window, as though remembering.

"In a hurry, I pulled away and felt a tug on my hair. Your necklace was caught in a curl. I'd broken it and heard the locket clatter to the deck. It popped open. I didn't know what to do, so I just froze." Charlotte rested her head on the chair but turned her face to me. "You went blurry, and seconds after you threw me a letter, you disappeared. I remember blinking a few times, wondering what I'd seen. You just weren't there.

I quickly grabbed the letter and shoved it into a pocket, then bent to get the locket just as Luke came around the corner with my mother.

"He took one look at the locket in my hand and lost all color as his eyes looked around. He was looking for you and he panicked. I really didn't know what to say. You disappeared before my eyes, and who would have believed an eight-year-old child if I'd told anyone. I was terrified. It took five, maybe ten minutes for the desperation in Luke's voice to get through to me.

"I told him I didn't know where you were. I'd told everyone that you were there one minute and gone the next. That was the truth." Charlotte wiped at a tear that was slowly sliding down her wrinkled cheek. "I didn't give Luke the letter."

"What?" I whispered in shock. "Why?" Ignoring the tears streaming down my own face, I waited. "Luke knew what happened to me. He did everything I told him to send me back to him."

Charlotte nodded. "When I was eighteen, I found the letter and realized I had to make sure it was delivered. It was ten years late in reaching your husband, but it reached him."

"Are you saying that you were really in 1912?" Niall asked, sitting forward.

"She was there," Charlotte told Niall. She turned

her eyes to me. "I know I should have given him the letter before we left the ship. Luke was desperate to find you. The ship was searched from top to bottom. I don't know what happened after that, but I've never forgotten the look on Luke's face when he realized you were gone.

"He loved you, Esmé. I found a love like that when I was in my early twenties." She smiled softly. "Niall Fionn McCormick was a distant cousin. He swept me off my feet. I didn't care that we had a loose family connection. I fell in love with him the first day we met. I miss him." She looked at Niall.

"I miss him too, Mom," Niall leaned forward and took his mother's hand. "He was a good father."

"Yes, he was." She smiled fondly. "He's been gone for many years. No one else ever interested me. It was him or no one. And I was okay with that. You only have a love like that once." Her eyes wandered to me. "You must find a way back to Luke."

I smiled through my tears. "I don't know how, because I left the necklace and locket behind."

Charlotte nodded slightly. "I'm going to take a nap, but I want you to visit the lady in the next room before you go."

I frowned and turned to see if Niall had any idea why. He shrugged and stood. "There's only one room she spends time in and it's to the left when we leave."

About to follow Niall out of the room, I looked back at Charlotte. I quickly walked over to the child I remembered and kissed her forehead. "Thank you," I whispered.

"I DON'T UNDERSTAND WHY SHE WOULD WANT ME TO visit one of her friends." I nervously reached out and knocked on the door.

When we heard a mumbled, "Come in," Niall opened the door and led me inside. He nearly knocked me over when I suddenly stopped in the doorway. My gaze was fixed on the elderly woman sitting in the chair by the window.

I could only vaguely hear Niall speaking.

It couldn't be. Could it?

"It's like seeing a ghost," the woman whispered, holding out a frail hand to me. "Come closer so I don't think I'm going crazy."

My legs trembled as I made my way across the room. I felt frail and as if I had aged those seventy-five years in just a few moments. I took my friend's hand

and sat beside her. "I never thought I'd see you again." I sobbed softly into a handful of tissues as Violet patted my hand.

"Holly, would you hand me the photo, please?" Violet asked, waving to the woman in the room, "This is my great-granddaughter Holly with her three children." I watched as she stared at Niall. "And you are Niall McCormick. Older than the last time I saw you."

I chuckled and tried to hide it, but Niall caught me and grinned, a slight blush on his cheeks. He coughed. "Violet, it's good to see you again. As pretty as ever."

The dress Violet wore was made of navy-blue silk and looked out of time. She had a dark and light blue knitted shawl around her shoulders to keep the chill at bay.

"Grandma, we're going, but I'll be back tomorrow. Alone, okay?" Holly said, kissing Violet's cheek.

"I'm sorry for interrupting your visit," I offered.

"It was time for us to go anyway, so please don't worry about it. These three need feeding." Holly smiled and led her three young children out of the room.

Violet sighed. "I love that girl, but she has her hands full." She turned to me and slowly handed me the photograph she'd asked Holly to pass her.

"Oh," I cried. "Luke," my voice broke as I stared at

my wedding photograph. "I've only been away from him for a few days, and I miss him so much."

Niall leaned over my shoulder, and I heard him gasp as he took a closer look. "This is you," he whispered. "All that with my mother and now Violet. It's all true."

"Yes," Violet confirmed, her eyes never leaving me.

"You disappeared on the Carpathia as it sailed into New York Harbor," Niall thought aloud. "Is that why they fished you out of the water? When you left in 1912 there was a ship where you were, but when you landed in 1987 there wasn't."

"I think so, but," I said, frowning, "when I left here, I was in my apartment in Manhattan, and I ended up on the Titanic just as it was leaving Southampton. I don't understand the how or the why of it all. I just know that I was there. And I love Luke. This is real." My eyes went back to the photograph in my hands. "How do I get back to you?" she asked Luke, stroking his face on the black and white image.

Niall said, "I'm a little confused as to how you managed to get from then to now, or vice versa. It makes no sense when I never thought it was possible to travel through time."

"It's a mystery that will never be solved," Violet

whispered. "But I never thought I'd see you again," she told me, her voice full of wonder.

Heartbroken, I said, "I don't know what to do with my life now. In a very short time, Luke became every-thing to me, and the thought of going on without him —I just can't."

"Would you go back to him if there was a way?" Niall asked.

I could see that the detective thought he'd lost his mind along with us. I smiled reassuringly. If he was crazy, he was in good company. "I would go back to him in a heartbeat if I could. All I know is that the clothes and the locket were the trigger for me. I don't have either." I stood and walked to the window, clutching the photograph to my chest.

Outside, the snow swirled in the wind, and I had no idea what to do. The life I wanted was gone, as was my husband.

My breath caught in my throat, and I didn't even try to stop the tears from streaming down my cheeks. The loss was so great that I didn't know how to go on. I didn't want to be in my old life. I didn't belong here anymore. Body and soul longed for what I had left in the past, and without Luke in my life, I didn't even want to wake up the next day.

How could I ever explain my feelings? I couldn't

because no one would ever understand. They probably wouldn't believe me either.

"Esmé," Niall said, reaching out to her. "You're freezing." He grabbed a blanket Violet had pointed to and wrapped it around my shoulders. "Come and sit down." He smiled. "I seem to be saying that a lot today."

I smiled through my tears and patted his arm. "You're a good man, Niall McCormick."

"My wife always thought so." His sad words drew my attention to his face. I searched and found a blank expression before he sighed heavily. "She died six years ago."

"You still miss her?"

"Every day," he admitted.

I squeezed his wrist and sat down next to Violet. "I don't know what to do anymore."

"You need to talk to John." Violet broke the silence. "He always knew more than he ever told anyone, including Luke after you disappeared. I had a feeling he knew where you were, but when I asked him, he said he knew as much as we did. I never believed him.

"I've seen him over the years, and the last time I saw him, he looked as young as he did when we all met, so many years ago now." Violet frowned. "He can do the same as you?" She stared directly at me.

It was true, and there was no reason why I couldn't admit who John was. "John was born in the 1700s and kept appearing on the Titanic. He didn't know why or how. All he told me was that I couldn't say a word to anyone about what I knew. If I did, I'd be transported back to my time. The Titanic would still sink, and no one on board would remember me.

"A big part of me was selfish, because I never wanted Luke to forget me, and the other part knew that I wouldn't be able to make a difference." I offered a wry smile. "You see, John wasn't supposed to be on the lifeboat we used to leave the ship. He simply refused to go down with the ship again. I don't think he was supposed to survive, but he did. I always knew he wasn't telling me everything, but I really don't think it was about time travel. I think it was more about the future," my voice softened and trailed off as I really thought about it.

"What if John knows what is happening now?" I moved to the edge of my seat as the words tumbled out of my mouth. "He might be able to take me back to Luke, or he might know a way for me to get back without the locket." I took Violet's hands. "Do you know where he is?"

"No. I haven't seen him in years, but I wonder—" Violet glanced out the window before meeting my gaze. "Jake and Sienna were here asking for information about you. Something tells me that your future lies with them and William."

Painfully, I admitted, "I was engaged to Jake and broke it off rather abruptly just before I disappeared. I don't love him, and I'm not sure I ever did. He deserves someone to love him the way I love Luke." I inhaled. "He's a good man, but he's not Luke."

"Then don't worry about him, because I think he's in love with Sienna." Violet smiled. "He was very concerned about her when we talked, and I may be old, but I'm certainly not blind." She smiled. "Go to your friends. Ask them if you can go through Luke's things. There might be something there."

"I will." I sat back and looked at Niall when I had a sudden thought. "Why wasn't I on the list of survivors?"

"What do you mean?" Niall asked.

"When I was researching Luke and the Titanic, I checked the passenger list and there was no Esmé Carlisle or Esmé Rogers on the list. When I boarded the Carpathia, I gave my name as Esmé Carlisle, or rather Luke did. I would have noticed if my name was next to his because they were alphabetical. So why wasn't my name there? That doesn't make any sense."

Niall sighed, "Maybe because you disappeared before you docked in New York."

"No, they got your name wrong." Violet shook her head. "On the list of survivors, which I saw, just like Luke, your name was listed as Esmé Lyle. Luke tried to get it changed, but they wouldn't change it without you. They flat out refused. He was so angry.

"I hope you find your way back to him, Esmé. You both deserve to be together." She smiled sadly. "I will be with my James before the New Year. I'm looking forward to it. I've had a good life, but I need to be with my husband now."

After a glance at Niall, who looked as choked up as I felt, I leaned forward and kissed Violet on the forehead. "Thank you and say hello to James for me." I paused. "If you see Luke, tell him I love him very much." My voice cracked.

[illegible]
[illegible]
[illegible]
[illegible]
[illegible]
[illegible]
[illegible]
[illegible]
[illegible]
[illegible]
[illegible]
[illegible]
[illegible]
[illegible]
[illegible]
[illegible]

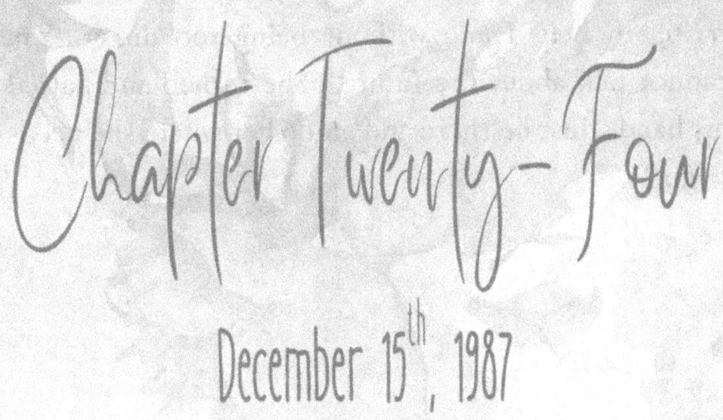

"LET ME JUST ASK MY MOM SOMETHING," NIALL SAID as they left Violet's room.

"I'll wait in reception." Esmé smiled and left.

Niall took a deep breath and pushed his way into his mother's room.

She turned her sleepy eyes to his and smiled. "I knew you wouldn't let it go. You always were a curious child."

"I accept what you, Violet and Esmé have said as the truth, whatever you believe it to be. I don't know how, but what haven't you told Esmé?"

With a knowing look on her face, Charlotte turned to the window. "Everything has a meaning, and we're trying to help Esmé without being too direct. You cannot talk about the future." She turned and patted his hand. "Just be there and guide her where she needs to go."

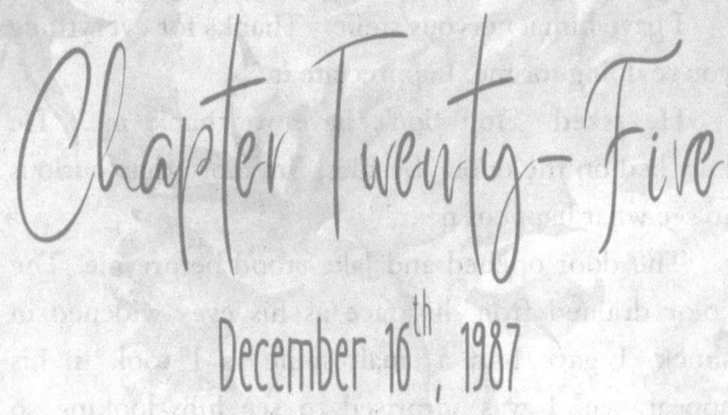

THE HEAT WAS ON IN NIALL'S CAR, BUT I STILL FELT chilled to the bone. I hadn't talked much since we had left the residential home the day before. There was not much for me to say anyway. My throat felt raw, and my eyes were swollen with emotion. Nothing felt or tasted the same without Luke. It was like he had died all over again.

Niall parked on the street in front of the house where everything had really started for Esmé - Luke's home.

A thick layer of snow covered the wrought iron railing in front of the large townhouse.

As Niall opened the car door for me, he helped me onto the sidewalk. "It's icy. Be careful."

I gave him a nervous smile. "Thanks for everything you're doing for me. I appreciate it."

He tsked. "You don't have to thank me." He knocked on the door. "Besides, I'm more than curious to see what happens next."

The door opened and Jake stood before me. The color drained from his face as his eyes widened in shock. I gave him a small smile as I took in his appearance. I was surprised to see him looking so disheveled; his hair needed brushing, his shirt hung from the waist of his jeans. He cleared his throat and reached for me. "I thought I saw things." He pulled me into a brief embrace and motioned for Niall to enter.

Niall quickly closed the door to keep the snow from trampling everywhere.

"Sienna!" Jake shouted and then looked uncertain - almost nervous.

"I know about you and Sienna, and I'm happy for you both." I patted his hand and accepted my friend's warm hug.

"We've been looking all over for you." Sienna looked at Jake. "Without much success, I might add."

"I'll explain as best I can, but I need your help." I took Sienna's hand. "Will you both help me?" I begged.

"If we can," Jake replied. "Of course, we'll help you." He turned to Niall.

I vaguely heard them introduce themselves as Sienna led me into the living room. "Did you really go back to Luke?" Sienna asked before we had a chance to sit down.

Niall sat down next to me, and I slowly told my story. There wasn't a dry eye in the room when I finished. "I need to find John. Hopefully he'll know how to get me back to Luke. I need to be with him."

"I don't know anyone named John." Sienna frowned and looked at Jake.

He shook his head. "It's not a name we've come across in our search for more information about Luke and you."

"What about the attic?" Niall suggested. "Wouldn't there be papers up there that belonged to Luke, especially since he owned this house back then?"

"We were in the attic, looking for clues about you," Jake told me. "But we didn't find much."

The disappointment Jake felt at not being able to help me was evident in the slump of his shoulders. His frown deepened as his eyes landed on Sienna.

Tears hovered on Sienna's face, and as all eyes focused on me, a voice behind us said, "There might be papers at the other house."

Sienna blinked and stood quickly. "Niall, this is William. He was adopted by Luke when he was two years old." She turned to me. "You remember him?"

I nodded.

"Hello, everyone." He waved and knit his bushy eyebrows together in deep concentration. "I don't think anyone's been here in years. One man," he paused, "Jonathan, looks after the place. Has done for a long time."

I gasped. "Jonathan! Could that be John?" My excitement grew.

"I don't remember anything about another house, and why wasn't it in all the papers the lawyer had?" Sienna asked. "I was there with you and your son," she told William.

"Hmm," he mumbled, not meeting her gaze as he added, "I don't remember," which told me that he knew more than he was saying. I glanced at Niall, who raised an eyebrow.

William continued, "There's a house in Stowe, Vermont that belongs to my father. I'll find you the address." He walked away, deep in thought.

"I really hope he hasn't let his imagination run away with him," Sienna added quietly. "He's done it once or twice before."

"He seemed sincere," Niall observed. "Though I think he knows more than he's letting on."

"Maybe," Jake began, "that place in Stowe holds the key to what happened." He shrugged. "Someone, somewhere, has to know."

William reappeared with a piece of paper in his hand. "I have the address." He sat down and faced me.

William shifted uncomfortably.

"Anyway, I think we are going to visit the house in Vermont." Sienna took my hand and squeezed it.

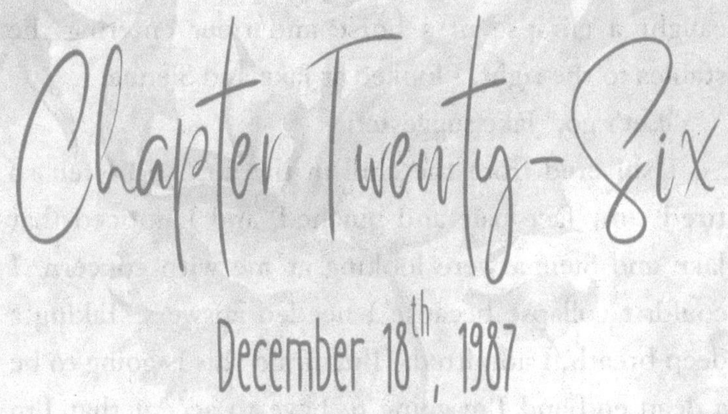

Chapter Twenty-Six

December 18th, 1987

THE LARGE HOUSE WAS SET BACK FROM THE MAIN road by a curved driveway. It was difficult to see many features of the landscape because of the heavy snow-fall from the night before. Everything was blanketed in a heavy whiteness that was almost comforting. It was quiet and serene, and not really what I had expected. Although I hadn't given much thought to what kind of house Luke would own, I had just made it my business to find him.

Jake stopped the car outside as we sat and looked around. Niall had stayed behind in New York with his sister, though his curiosity was piqued.

There was no movement from the house, but I

caught a glimpse of a horse and rider entering the stables to the right. I looked at Jake and Sienna.

"Let's go," Jake suggested.

I shivered from the chill in the air. And I felt so tired - my face pale and pinched, and I noticed that Jake and Sienna were looking at me with concern. I couldn't collapse because I needed answers. Taking a deep breath, I admitted, "I'm afraid this is going to be a dead end and I'm going to have to accept that I'm never going to see Luke again." My voice cracked as I felt an acute sense of loss.

Sienna took my hand and held on as we walked toward the barn. The snow crunched under our boots as we approached the tall double doors. The sound of a latch being inserted from the inside, followed by a splash of water, drew my gaze to the left. I caught the glimpse of the back of a man just before we heard the muffled thud of horse hooves as he led the horse to the water trough. Seconds later, the horse began to drink, and the man realized he wasn't alone.

His heavy sigh was heard at the door. "What can I do for you?" As he turned, I gasped.

It wasn't John.

As he approached, I guessed he was in his fifties, over six feet tall with broad shoulders and a slim waist. He cleared his throat. "What's going on?"

"I'm sorry," I stumbled over my words. "Is this the Carlisle place?"

"Who wants to know?" He crossed his arms and waited, but I didn't miss the recognition in his eyes before he blinked quickly, and it was gone.

I glanced at Jake and Sienna and realized they had decided this was my show. I swallowed. "I'm Esmé Carlisle."

The man didn't look surprised. "I never thought —" he shook his head before running a hand through his hair. "I never thought I would meet you."

I frowned. "I don't understand. Are you Jonathan?"

"Yes." He smiled. "My father always spoke fondly of you."

"John," I whispered.

"He was a good man. Unlike most." Jonathan smiled and motioned for us to follow him to the house. "Who are you two?" he asked, looking at Jake and Sienna.

They introduced themselves as he led us into the cozy kitchen. "I don't live in this house because it's yours," he said to me, "but I look after it and keep some supplies here for when I work long days."

"Belongs to me?" I rubbed my forehead, a headache forming.

"How long has the house been Esmé's?" Sienna inquired, giving me only a quick glance.

"About sixty years, I think. It was before I was born anyway." He poured us coffee without even asking if we'd like some. "My father talked about you," he told me. "He always said he wouldn't have had the life he had if you hadn't helped him change his future." He took a sip of the hot coffee, too hot for me. "It took me a long time to understand what he meant."

"Did you ever meet Luke?" Jake asked.

Jonathan paused and let the silence settle before admitting, "Yes, I did. That was all he offered.

"Was he alone?" Jake persisted.

Jonathan looked at me and hesitated before answering, "Yes."

He was lying. Why?

The silence was painful. Knowing that Luke had been in the house with another woman hurt. It hurt more than I could bear. In a hurry, I stood quickly. "I shouldn't be here. I have to go."

A hand reached out and grabbed her wrist. "Wait," Jonathan snapped. "I never said who he was with, so don't jump to conclusions."

With a shaking hand, I wiped the tears from my eyes. "I just want to be with him. It has been six days since I last saw him, and when he died," I paused to control the sobs that were about to break out, "he had been without me for over seventy years. I want to get back to him and be by his side. I just don't know how."

Jonathan held my gaze and took my wrist. "I need to talk to you alone." He turned to Jake and Sienna. "There are sandwiches and cake in the refrigerator. Help yourself to those and more coffee." He finally let go of me and motioned for me to follow him out of the house. "It's cold out here, but I have to take you somewhere." He looked at my feet. "At least you have proper shoes on."

Large snowflakes fell as he led me around the back of the house and toward the line of trees farther back from the property. I hesitated and looked at him, uneasiness creeping up her spine.

He offered a wry smile. "Don't be afraid. I'm not going to hurt you. Just send you back to Luke."

I stumbled and stared. "What?" I whispered. "How?"

He turned to face her. "I'm not one to talk or be around other people. I like it that way. All I know is what my father told me to do if you ever showed up here. He always knew more than Luke, which would cause big fights between them. My father knew everything." Jonathan grinned.

He left me in his wake. I ran as fast as I could in

the thick snow so I wouldn't lose sight of him. We went through the trees and walked for more than twenty minutes before Jonathan took my arm and stopped.

"I can't go any further." He turned me to face him. "If you go through the two trees behind me, keep going. You'll know when you are no longer in 1987." He looked away. "Please don't ask me how or why because I don't know. I think my father did, but he never told me."

He looked back at the trees and then turned to me. "I was told to tell you that when you return, you will have been missing for four years. It will be 1916. But Esmé, when you go back, you stay in the past. There are no more triggers. Nothing. This is your one chance to be with Luke for the rest of your life. Do you understand me?"

"Yes." Was that the truth? Could it really be that easy for me to be with my husband again? "Will I be able to tell him the truth about what happened to me?"

He nodded, a small smile playing on his lips. "Yes. You'll be there permanently."

I took a moment to consider his words and then, before I could think, I hugged Jonathan, much to his surprise, and ran toward the two trees he'd indicated.

The snow frustrated me, but my desperation to get back to Luke won out over every obstacle. Then I stood between the two trees. The sound of a swarm of bees buzzing around my head grew louder and I stopped and turned to face Jonathan. I watched him fall to the ground before the image of him faded. I also fell to the cold snow as the dizziness grew stronger and bolder. Everything went black for a moment, and then I felt as if I were falling, seconds before everything around me went silent - still.

Chapter Twenty-Seven

July 12th, 1916

THE GROUND BENEATH ME NO LONGER FELT COLD and wet. Instead, it was hard and warm. I looked up and let the sun's rays warm my face before slowly opening my eyes and looking around. If it weren't for the fact that the snow had disappeared, I would think I hadn't gone anywhere. But I was in another season now. The sun broke through the branches of the trees, warming me completely in my winter jacket and thick boots.

A tree root dug into my buttocks as I slowly used the trunk of a tree to guide myself to my feet. My legs felt unsteady, and my head swam before my eyes stopped blurring. Did I dare to believe that I had made it? Had I really come back to find Luke?

Before my brain could follow, I started walking back the way I'd come with Jonathan. He was nowhere in sight. My legs gained strength as I picked up speed, almost tripping over the roots of the trees. Of course, they'd been buried under thick snow the first time I'd taken the path.

At the first sight of the house, I stumbled to a halt and grabbed a branch to keep from falling to the ground. The house looked the same, though I could see that it was painted a pale yellow with white trim. It looked and felt quiet, as if no one was there. I prayed I was wrong.

Slowly moving forward, I glanced to my left and felt the skin on the back of my neck tingle as if I were being watched. I shook it off and walked around to the front of the house.

Why was it so quiet?

My heart raced as I glanced at the front door before slowly pulling it open and stepping inside. Someone had to be home.

A sudden noise from the kitchen caught me mid-step, so I took a chance and called out, "Luke?"

The noise stopped.

"Luke?" I called louder, seconds before I heard a crash followed by a curse.

I ran to the kitchen and caught an angry "I'm

imagining her again," muttering under his breath. I watched as he fell to his knees, his shoulders slumped as he began to shake. He fell onto his butt, which caused me to move.

Luke must have sensed the movement because he looked up and smiled through his tears. "I see you even when I'm awake now."

"No," I said, dropping down to take his hands in mine. Tears streamed down my face unchecked as I watched Luke stare at me. "I'm real, Luke." I climbed onto his lap and wrapped my arms around his neck. I tightened around him in an embrace that I never wanted to end. "I never wanted to leave. It was an accident I'll tell you about later." I kissed his ear, his neck, and finally cupped his face in my trembling hands. "I am real, Luke. Touch me. Feel me. I love you."

"Esmé," he breathed my name against my lips as he cupped my face. He swallowed hard.

"I promise," I kissed his palm, "that I am as real as you are."

His fingers gradually caressed my eyes, my cheekbones, and hovered over my lips. "Why did you leave me? Where did you go?"

I gasped through my tears. "It was out of my control." I smiled. "I will tell you everything, but first

I need you to hold me. Promise me that no matter how crazy my story sounds, you will believe me."

Suddenly embraced in Luke's strong arms, I gave in to my relief and sank into my husband. He meant more to me than anyone, and I was afraid that I would wake up and find it all a dream.

"Do you think you can stand?" I asked, moving away from Luke. I held out a hand to him.

"What are you wearing?" he asked, staring at my jacket.

I took it off. "I'll explain later."

He paused and nodded. "I never gave up hope that you would find your way back to me," he admitted, intertwining our fingers. "Let me show you, our room." He offered a shy smile.

Upstairs, the master bedroom at the front of the house was spacious and comfortable. Luke watched as I took my time walking around the room, taking it all in. A sideboard off to one side held pictures of them from the Titanic in beautiful frames.

A white bedspread with little rosebuds covered the bed. On the small table on Luke's side of the bed was a smaller wedding photograph.

"I haven't really lived without you." The wedding ring on Luke's finger caught my attention as he ran his hands through his hair.

At that moment, nothing else mattered but them. I threw my sweater across the room and reached for Luke.

"Make love to me," I breathed against his lips, seconds before his mouth covered mine hungrily. His kiss was urgent and searching. As he carried me to the bed, I felt like I was floating on air.

Luke trembled as he lifted his mouth from mine and looked intensely into my eyes. "I love you, Esmé. Only you. Always. I have never stopped."

He captured my lips and crushed me beneath him. I didn't care. I had missed him and never wanted to be separated from him again.

A trail of fire followed his lips as they moved down my neck to my chest. "I don't know what this is, but I like it," he growled, referring to the stretchy tank top I wore.

Large hands gently outlined the circle of my breasts, causing them to swell at the intimacy. His head dipped as he nibbled at the sensitive nipples poking through her top.

I wrapped my legs around his hips, wanting to feel Luke's hardness.

He suddenly tore off my top, letting it sail through the air as he moaned at the sight of my bare, quivering breasts. With an unsteady hand, he unfastened my jeans and pulled them, along with my panties, down my legs. He quickly removed his own clothes and lowered his body over mine.

Our mutual gasps of excitement were lost as blood rushed through my ears. Luke was everywhere. Consuming all of me. I couldn't get enough of him as my hands ran down his back to the firm cheeks of his bottom. He shivered at my touch. He cursed as I slid a hand between us, wrapping my fingers around the hard flesh between his legs.

"Love me," I pleaded, pulling him closer so we could join.

He plunged into me and hissed, "Always."

He held still, his breath as heavy as mine. Our eyes locked as he slowly began to make love to me.

Tears rolled down my cheeks as Luke placed a tender kiss on each of my breasts.

I ran my fingers through the back of his hair and brought his mouth to mine. His eyes glazed over as his mouth parted and he kissed me as if he were devouring me.

He aroused me beyond the point of return as I surrendered completely to the passion Luke created with the slide of his flesh and the feel of our bodies rubbing together.

My body began to vibrate with liquid fire, and as I

held Luke's gaze, a tremor inside me heated my thighs and groin, driving me to a climax beyond anything I had ever experienced. Eyes closed, I gasped. Straining against Luke, I felt him reach completion as well.

Time seemed to move in slow motion until Luke scooped me up in his arms and held me against his chest, our legs intertwined.

"You're wearing my locket," I said, fingering the object that had brought me to Luke in the first place. I felt it on my chest when Luke made love to me.

"I've never taken it off since I had it repaired. I have no plans to."

"I'm so sorry, Luke." I kissed his shoulder.

Quietly, with his fingers making circles on my back, Luke asked, "Did John know you were coming back to me today?"

The hand on his chest stopped moving and I lifted my eyes to his. "I haven't spoken to him, but he knows everything." I closed my eyes and kissed his chest. "Tell me why you're asking, and I'll tell you everything about me and how I disappeared from the Carpathia."

I rested my chin on his chest and felt delight at the gentle brush of his fingers on my shoulder. "John lives here, and he told me I had to be here today. He was insistent."

"How did John end up here?"

He raised an eyebrow at me for asking another question when I had promised only one. He answered anyway, "When we couldn't find you on the ship, something told me to keep John close. He had nowhere else to go, so he came with me. At first I thought he was in love with you, but then he admitted that the only feelings he had for you were sisterly." He smiled. "In the end, John was the only one I could talk to about you."

Luke closed his eyes and breathed in. "I missed you. Every second of every day, Esmé."

"This time I'm not going anywhere unless it's with you." I moved closer and buried my face in his neck. "Let me tell you what happened to me—"

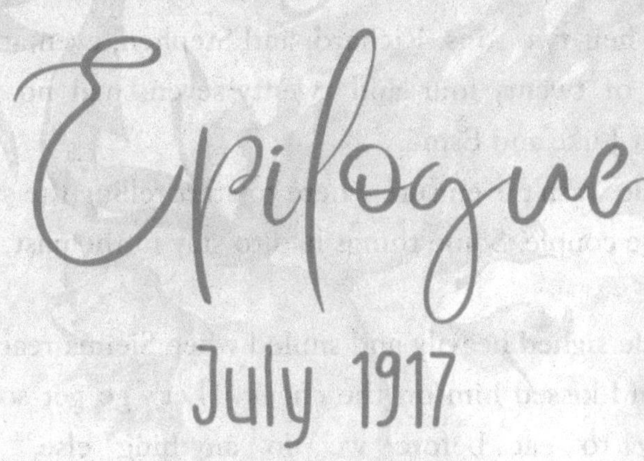

JAKE STOOD WITH HIS ARM AROUND HIS WIFE OF twenty-nine years as they watched the moving truck pull away. It had taken both Sienna and him by surprise when the letter arrived from the Boston attorneys. Bequeathed to them by a Jonathan John Sutter. The Jonathan they'd met thirty years ago - and never spoken to since.

Sienna had insisted that Esmé had something to do with the bequest. Perhaps she had.

Years had passed since they had both last seen Esmé, and it was in the very house they were the new owners of in Stowe.

Jake had wondered about Esmé over the years, but he and Sienna had agreed to stop looking into the past. It had been hard to let go at first, but their lives had moved on. And it had become easier.

Their two sons, Richard, and Stephen, even at the ages of twenty-four and twenty-seven, had no idea about Luke and Esmé.

He wasn't even sure where to start telling the story of the couple. Some things had to stay in the past, like Esmé.

He sighed heavily and smiled when Sienna reached up and kissed him on the cheek. "Let's go get something to eat before we do anything else," she suggested.

They walked into the house and found their sons in the kitchen. Many old photographs were spread across the table.

"Look what Rich found in the back of the closet in the master bedroom," Stephen said excitedly. "They were in an old shoebox."

Jake sat down heavily in a chair as shock ran through him. He recognized the woman in many of the pictures.

"Oh," Sienna joined them at the table and selected a picture. "It can't be—" her voice trailed off.

"You can't know her, Mom. The back of the one you're holding is dated 1922," Richard commented, frowning. "Mom?" He looked at his father. "Dad?"

Jake flipped through the pictures and began to laugh

through the tears that were streaming from his eyes and down his face. He took Sienna's hand. "She found a way to let us know that she had a life with Luke."

Sienna nodded as they continued to look at the photographs. They told a story they hadn't even imagined.

"This looks like it was taken in Ireland," Stephen said, turning the picture over. "Cobh, 1928."

"And this," Richard said. "Disneyland, July 1955."

Jake gently took the photo from his son and wiped his eyes. "I think that must be William and his wife, and is that, David?" Jake pointed to Sienna.

"It must be," she whispered.

Moments later, Sienna gasped. "Look, she lived to be an old lady." Sienna held up a 1985 photo of Esmé and Luke. Sienna cried.

"You two are not making much sense," Stephen grumbled.

Richard chuckled. "They never do."

Jake glanced at Sienna before they turned to their sons, who were watching them closely. "I think," Jake smiled, "it's time your mother and I told you about Esmé and Luke Carlisle, because I don't think they want to stay in the past any longer."

The End

Thank you for reading Come Back to Me by Lexi Buchanan.

Dear Reader

Thank you for reading *Come Back to Me,* and thank you for your reviews! It's really appreciated.

Subscribe with your email to be alerted about new releases, sales, and events.
www.lexibuchanan.com

Other books by Author

Hawke's Ridge

Maddox (2025)

Den Hollows

One of Six · Two of Six (2025)

Den of Filth (New MC Series 2025)

Reckless Wilder (2026)

Fifth Realm Series (Romantasy)

Quiver of Chaos · Wings & Arrows (2026)

Standalone Romantasy

Persephone Unchained

Tallulah James Mystery

*Dead and a Murder or Two · Dead and the Wedding Crashers ·
Dead and a Deadly Deed · Dead and a Best Friend*

Boston Bay Vikings

*Camden · Bennett · Ethan · Sutton · Carter · Bryson · Ivan · Theo ·
Noah · Knox · Jericho · Roman*

Boston Bay Vikings Minor League

Lake · Rhodes · Nikoli · Dario · Madden · Bradford

Single Titles

Butterflies and Darkness · *Come Back to Me* · *Indecent Villain* · *Lawful* · *Love Stryker* · *Tears in the Rain* · *Whispers of Yesterday*

Holiday Season

Holiday Kisses in the Snow · *Jingle Bells*

Romantic Suspense Series

Twenty Eight Days · *The Next Victim (2025)*

Blossom Creek

Christmas at Emelia's · *A Rake in Blossom Creek* · *Heatwave in Blossom Creek* · *Secret Love in Blossom Creek* · *Mischief in Blossom Creek* · *Runaway Bride in Blossom Creek* · *Naughty & Nice in Blossom Creek*

Bad Boy Rockers

My Brother's Girl · *Past Sins* · *My Best Friend's Sister* · *Never Let Go* · *Saving Jace* · *Silent Night (Novella)*

Kincaid Sisters

Meant to be Mine · *You Were Always Mine* · *Will You be Mine*

McKenzie Brothers

Playing with the Boss · *A McKenzie Wedding (Novella)* · *Playing with Fire* · *Playing with Desire* · *Playing with Trouble* · *Playing with their Hearts* · *A McKenzie Christmas (Novella)*

De La Fuente Family (McKenzie Spinoff)

Love in Montana · *Love in Purgatory* · *Love in Bloom* · *Love in Country* · *Love in Flame* · *Love in Game* · *Love in Education*

McKenzie Cousins

(McKenzie Spinoff)

Baby Makes Three · A Business Decision · Secret Kisses · Kissing Cousins · If Only · Princess & the Puck · A Bakers Delight · A Cowboy for Christmas · A Secret Affair · One Christmas · The Pregnant Professor · It Started with a Kiss

Novella's

Educate Me · One Dance · Pure

About the Author

While Lexi is the author of the chick lit series, Tallulah James Mystery, and the sexy wild Alaska series, Hawke's Ridge, she also writes romantasy. This author has over seventy published novels. Based in Ireland, this British author has been writing since 2013.

Follow on social media:

Website: www.lexibuchanan.com
Email: authorlexibuchanan@gmail.com

facebook.com/lexibuchananauthor
x.com/AuthorLexi
instagram.com/authorlexib
bookbub.com/author/lexi-buchanan
amazon.com/Lexi-Buchanan/e/B009SPA94U